The Diamond Hills

By
Helen Fain

PublishAmerica
Baltimore

© 2007 by Helen Fain.
All rights reserved. No part of this book may be reproduced, stored in a retrieval system or transmitted in any form or by any means without the prior written permission of the publishers, except by a reviewer who may quote brief passages in a review to be printed in a newspaper, magazine or journal.

First printing

PublishAmerica has allowed this work to remain exactly as the author intended, verbatim, without editorial input.

All characters in this book are fictitious, and any resemblance to real persons, living or dead, is coincidental.

ISBN: 1-60441-551-7
PUBLISHED BY PUBLISHAMERICA, LLLP
www.publishamerica.com
Baltimore

Printed in the United States of America

Chapter 1

Little seven-year-old Jake Stevens watched as the moving truck pulled up into the drive of the two story house that was just down the street from where he lived. Somebody was moving into his neighborhood. From a distance of a hundred yards, he straddled his bike and stared as two burly men hopped out of the vehicle, opened the back hatch and began hauling boxes out. It was a small moving truck, with the logo of an unknown moving company emblazed on both sides. "They must not have a lot of stuff," Jake thought to himself, referring to whoever was moving in. Maybe, the new family would have a little boy his age. It would be nice to have someone to play with.

Suddenly, the sound of a muffler rumbled from down the street. Jake saw an old, blue pickup truck idling towards the house, its bed carrying a few green lawn bags and boxes. The vehicle looked pretty beat up. Jake smirked. At least it would fit into the neighborhood. Nobody around here drove fancy cars. The truck pulled up to the curb and stopped in front of the bare yard that had little grass and tons of weeds. A man got out. Even from a distance, Jake could see that the man looked gruff and irritated. Without smiling, he walked up to the movers who were carrying boxes. He began talking and pointing towards the boxes and then towards the house. "That must be the dad," thought Jake. Did he have a family? Jake looked back towards the pickup and saw one other person sitting on the passenger side. It looked like a little kid, maybe his age. The kid opened the door and got out. Jake strained his eyes to see who it was. "Oh shoot!" Jake said out loud. The kid had a long pony tail. "A stupid girl!" he muttered under his breath. Nonetheless, he stayed and watched as the girl stood there and looked at her new house. She didn't wear a frilly little dress like most girls did. Instead, she wore blue jean overalls and tennis shoes. If it hadn't have been for that long, brown ponytail, she would have almost passed for a boy. Jake wondered if she was seven too. The gruff, irritated man walked back towards the pickup and handed the girl a box to haul in. She stood there motionless, still staring at the house as if she was not ready to call it home. The dad grabbed a couple of the lawn bags and headed towards the front door. Seeing that his daughter was not following his lead, he angrily hollered for her to come into the house. She reluctantly did as she was told. Jake pulled his baseball cap lower onto his head. "So much for having someone to play with," thought Jake. He hopped onto his bike and headed up the street.

Chapter 2

Chloe Mayer threw the baseball high up into the air and caught it. She scuffed her shoes as she slowly made her way up the street, not bothering to walk on the cracked sidewalks that stretched from one end of this new neighborhood to the other. The sun was hot on her shoulders. She was thirsty. But she wasn't about to go back into the house. Her dad was mad, again. He told her to go out and play. She was just in the way.

Chloe looked all around her. It was quiet here. As far as she knew, there were no other kids who laughed and played. Just old looking houses with ugly yards and neighbors that hardly spoke and certainly didn't smile at you. She hated this place. But Daddy said they had to move. Mommy was gone now and they had to find a new life. Chloe missed her mom, even if her mom always cried. At least she was there. But now, Chloe just had Daddy. And Daddy always seemed mad.

Chloe continued walking. Out of nowhere, Chloe suddenly heard the sound of bicycle tires slowly crunching on gravel as this person came up behind her. She whirled around and saw a boy in a dirty baseball cap, balancing effortlessly on a dusty, black bike. He stared with brown eyes that mirrored her own. His face was smudged and sweaty, and the right knee of his jeans was ripped. "You scared me," she muttered.

The boy straddled his bike. "Are you the new kid?"

Chloe nodded her head yes.

"What's your name," he asked, not cracking a smile.

"Chloe. What's yours?" She watched as the boy spit on the street.

"Jake. I live right over there." He pointed to a house several houses down. "I'm seven."

"I'm seven too," she responded as she casually began tossing the baseball up in the air.

Jake stared at her for a second, as if he was trying to figure her out. "How come you don't play with dolls?"

Chloe frowned. "I don't like dolls."

Jake snorted. "You're a girl, aren't you? I thought all girls played with dolls and stupid stuff like that. And where's your girly dress?" He eyed her faded overalls and worn out shoes.

Chloe was getting angry. He was teasing her and being mean. "Well I'm not like that!" she hollered at him. She turned and began walking away. But he followed her until he was riding his bike slowly beside her.

"Where's your mom and dad?" he asked, not phased by the fact that he had just made her mad.

Chloe kept walking and tossing the ball. "Daddy's on the phone trying to get a job." She paused for a second. "And Mommy's *dead*." Up went the ball. And down it came again, back into Chloe's hands.

Jake stopped short on his bike. Chloe smirked, continuing to slowly walk up the street. She knew that would shut him up and make him leave her alone. It always did. He'd be just like all the other kids who thought Chloe was weird.

But to her surprise, he caught up with her once again. "My daddy died last Christmas," he stated plainly to her.

This time it was Chloe's turn to stop short. She gripped the ball tightly in her hands and turned to look at Jake.

Jake continued talking, speaking casually as if he had known Chloe forever. "He drank a lot. He was always gone. And then he got in a bad car accident. Now it's just me and Mom."

Chloe couldn't believe what she was hearing. She thought there was no one else in the world like her. Chloe looked up towards Jake's house. It didn't look like anyone was home. "Where's your mom?"

Jake shrugged. "Working."

Chloe looked back at Jake. "You stay home by yourself?" she asked, completely amazed.

"Yeah. It's no big deal." He spit another huge wad of saliva onto the ground. "I know how to make sandwiches. Mommy says we don't have enough money to pay someone to take care of me."

"Wow," was all Chloe could say. She wondered if she could stay home by herself too. Would she be scared?

Jake's eyes brightened suddenly. "Hey, wanna come over and play with my toy cars?" Jake asked.

Chloe nodded, instantly realizing she had someone to play with now. "Yeah! That would be fun." She followed Jake up the street towards his house.

Chapter 3

Slumped lazily on his sofa, Jake mindlessly flipped through the channels on the T.V. He heard his mom's car pull up into the drive. She walked in carrying a bag of groceries. He got up to help her, knowing that she expected it. He already knew too well that if he didn't, she'd start yelling and hitting. "Hi, Mommy," he softly replied.

"Hi," she replied dully, without even looking at him. He could tell she was tired. She always seemed tired. "What did you eat for lunch today?"

"Peanut butter and jelly," he responded as he put the bread up on the counter.

"You didn't get into trouble did you?" her voice already reflecting a tone of irritability.

"No."

"Good. You have to stay out of trouble. I can't be around to watch you." She opened the refrigerator to put the milk and eggs in.

"I know that," he responded.

She closed the refrigerator and looked at him. "Who are the people who moved in down the street several days ago?"

"A girl and her dad."

"No mom?" asked Jake's mother.

"No," was all Jake said.

Jake's mother grunted. "Hmmf. She probably left him for cheating on her. Stupid bastard."

His mother always made hasty assumptions. And so Jake decided not to tell her the truth. She wouldn't hear him anyway. She only heard what she wanted to hear.

Jake's mom wiped her brow. "Well, go take your shower while I get supper going." She pointed towards the hallway.

Jake placed the canned green beans on the counter and walked out of the kitchen.

His mother called after him. "Jake!"

He turned and looked at her.

She shook a finger at him. "You be careful getting to know these new people. I don't know how they would feel if they knew I left you alone during the day. God knows no one else around here gives a shit."

"I know, Mom," he softly responded again. He turned back around and headed towards the bathroom. Even at seven years old, he always felt that he shouldn't have to know to tread lightly, to watch his back. But little Jake certainly did.

Chapter 4

"Where the hell have you been?" Chloe's father hollered as she walked into the kitchen.

"Outside playing," she timidly replied.

"Who the hell with?" he barked. "It's getting dark outside."

"With that boy, Jake, I've been telling you about." Chloe watched as her dad quickly slapped some bologna between two slices of bread. He looked frazzled, a look she was getting used to seeing.

"Well, sit down," he growled. He pointed to the kitchen table. She did what he said. He plopped the plate down in front of her and sat down too. He rubbed his eyes.

Chloe looked down at her gross sandwich. She wasn't hungry. Casually, she slid the plate away.

Her dad groaned, still rubbing his eyes. "I got a job."

Chloe looked at him, puzzled. "That's good, isn't it?"

Her father leaned back against his chair. "It's in the mines, Chloe. I have to work at night…on the night shift."

"Oh," Chloe responded. She looked down at her sandwich again, not quite comprehending why her dad was so upset.

"What am I going to do with you?" he asked incredulously, more to himself than to her.

Chloe said nothing for a minute. And then she thought of Jake. "What about Jake's mom? She could watch me."

Chloe's father frowned. "Who?" he asked.

Chloe grew frustrated. Her dad never paid attention when she told him things. "Jake's mom. You know, up the street?"

He frowned even more, this time rubbing his temples. "I don't know."

Chloe picked at her dry sandwich. "Daddy. We don't know anybody else."

Her father stared off into space for what seemed like forever, leaning his chin on top of his clasped hands. Finally he stood up. "Ok. Let's go talk to her."

Chapter 5

Bill Mayer knocked on the door and waited. He looked down at his daughter who just simply looked back up at him with her big brown eyes. His head began to throb. Damn. Another migraine was coming on. It was the last thing he needed right now.

The door swung open and a woman stood there with a cigarette hanging from her lips. Bill quickly analyzed her dull blonde hair and her empty blue eyes, concluding that at one time, she was probably full of life and quite pretty. But now, she simply stared at him with a blank, tired expression on her face.

Bill cleared his throat to speak, only to be sidetracked suddenly by a little boy who appeared by his mother's side. Jake simply stared at Bill too. "Hello. I'm Bill Mayer, Chloe's dad." Bill contemplated extending his hand in a friendly gesture but at the last minute, decided against it. "We just moved in about a week ago." He motioned his head in the direction of his house.

She shifted from her left hip to her right hip but didn't change the blank expression on her face. "Yeah…so?" was all she said, the cigarette bobbing between her lips.

Bill figured she must have been as tired as he was. Or else she really didn't give a damn about him or who he was. He took a deep breath and sighed. "You're Jake's mom, right? Our kids have been playing together." He waited for her to introduce herself.

She must have finally got the sense to do just that. "Clarissa Stevens," was all she said and she took a long drag on her cigarette.

Bill decided to cut through the crap. "Look, I'm desperate here. We don't know anybody. I just got a job at the mines on the night shift. I gotta be there in an hour. I've got no one to watch Chloe. Would you mind?" He shoved Chloe in front of him as if seeing her might persuade Clarissa to liven up a bit and speed things along.

Clarissa continued to stare at him with her hollow eyes. And then she looked down at Chloe. "Stay the night?" she asked more to herself then to anyone else.

Bill glanced at his watch. Now he had 45 minutes to get to his new job. "Just until I figure something else out."

Clarissa took another drag on her cigarette and slowly blew the smoke out. "Yeah, sure. Why not?" She extended her arm out and flicked the ashes onto the porch right by Chloe's feet.

Bill breathed a sigh of relief. "Thank you. We'll go get her stuff and be right back." He grabbed Chloe's arm and pushed her out in front of him as they turned to leave. And then he turned back around. "I'll pay you when I get my first paycheck."

Clarissa dragged hard on her cigarette. "She's just going to be sleeping. So don't worry about it."

Bill tried his best to crack a smile. It was hard to. He didn't smile much these days. He rushed Chloe home and told her to throw some pajamas into a bag along with her toothbrush. Within five minutes they were back at Clarissa's door where Chloe eagerly walked into the living room, clutching her duffel bag close to her chest.

Bill looked at his watch again. 35 minutes to go. "Thanks again. I'll pick her up first thing in the morning."

Clarissa just nodded. It seemed she didn't have much to smile about these days either. He glanced down at Chloe and Jake. They were both grinning from ear to ear, obviously thrilled about the whole situation. Leave it to kids to always find the good in everything. Bill turned and headed back up the street towards his house.

Chapter 6

Clarissa Stevens poured herself another drink. How many was this? It didn't really matter. Because she savored the burn that she felt as the liquor went down her throat. And even better, she liked the buzz her head felt when the liquor took effect. Sitting at the kitchen table, she looked down at the pile of bills she was trying to sort through. Damn, she just couldn't do this tonight.

Sighing heavily, she picked up her drink and plopped down in the recliner in the living room. She stared at little Jake's school picture that sat on top of the T.V. That was the only picture in this whole stinkin' house. She used to have lots of pictures. Pictures of her when she was full of life – vibrant and beautiful. And pictures of *him*. Bruce. Her husband. Her lying, cheating, abusive, alcoholic husband. Clarissa grunted. Oh yeah, don't forget *dead*. She could add that adjective to the list as well. Lousy bastard. She wasn't enough for him. Jake wasn't enough for him. He had to go out and screw every whore in this godforsaken town. And to top it off, he had to go out drinking on Christmas Eve and slam his car into a telephone pole, leaving her alone to take care of Jake. To face this world with disgrace and embarrassment. She hated him. She hated all men. They were all absolutely worthless. God, life would be so much easier if she were all alone. She could just pick up and leave. Move far, far away where no one knew her or her past.

But she wasn't alone. She had Jake. Little Jake who looked just like his father. There wasn't a day when she didn't see him in little Jake. It was always there. A terrible reminder. She slugged back the rest of her drink.

Innocent little kid laughter came from the back bedroom; sounds that should make any mother smile. But Clarissa hated it. She had enough noise going on in her mind. She wanted peace and quiet. The laughter continued. And Clarissa's head began to pound. Just like it did every night at this time. She hollered vehemently towards the hallway. "You guys brush your teeth and get to bed!"

The laughter quickly stopped. "Ok, Mom," came Jake's voice. She heard the pitter patter of little feet making their way to the bathroom. That was the last sound Clarissa remembered hearing before she passed out into a deep, alcohol-induced sleep.

Chapter 7

Jake stared up at his ceiling, watching the shadows from the trees dance in the gentle breeze. "Are you asleep?" he whispered to Chloe who was lying on the floor in his Spiderman sleeping bag.

"No," she whispered back.

Jake got out of bed. "Come on then. I want to show you something." He grabbed his backpack from the closet and stuffed a flashlight and two old blankets in it.

Chloe sat up. "Where are we going?"

"Shhh!" he warned. "Wait right here. I'll be back." He slowly opened his bedroom door and peered out. Quietly, he crept down the hall and into the kitchen where he grabbed a box of cookies from the cabinet. Peeking in on his mom, he was relieved to see she was still fast asleep in her recliner. He stealthily crept back to his bedroom. "Get your shoes on. Let's go," he whispered.

Chloe did as Jake said and followed him out the door, being careful not to wake his mother in the process. Once outside and in the clear, Jake put his backpack on his back and hopped onto his bike. "Let's go get your bike."

"We're going to get in trouble."

"No we won't. I do this all the time. My mom never knows." They both made their way down the street towards Chloe's empty, dark house. She hopped onto her bike and followed Jake as they rode for what seemed like forever. They began heading up a winding, dirt road that led deep into the woods which stretched for miles behind their neighborhood. "Don't be scared, Chloe. It's just the woods."

Chloe didn't say anything. She just huffed and puffed as she pedaled with all of her might to keep up with Jake. Finally, Jake slowed down and then came to a complete stop. He threw his bike down on the ground and watched as Chloe did the same. "Where are we going?" she asked for the second time, trying to catch her breath.

"It's just right up here. Come on." The two kids walked a little ways further through thick pine trees and underbrush until they came to a clearing and a cliff that overlooked another clearing way down below.

"I've never been outside in the dark like this. What is this place?" asked Chloe.

Jake pointed down towards the clearing below. "Big kids go down there to drink beer and kiss and stuff."

Chloe wrinkled her nose. "That's gross."

"Yeah, I know," agreed Jake, wrinkling his own nose. He turned back around and looked at the small clearing they were standing in. "But this is *my* secret hiding place."

Chloe glanced around at the surrounding trees and listened to the millions of crickets that chirped in the darkness. "What's the name of this place?"

Jake opened his arms wide towards the rolling forest all around them. "This whole area…all of the surrounding woods…it's called 'The Diamond Hills'," he stated proudly. He suddenly felt so smart.

Chloe raised an eyebrow. "'The Diamond Hills'? Are there diamonds around here or something?"

Jake shook his head. "Not those kinds of diamonds." Jake pointed up towards the black sky. "*Those* kinds of diamonds."

Chloe arched her neck and looked up. She gasped. "Wow," she whispered. A billion, quadrillion stars sparkled back at her. She had never seen anything like it. "They do look like diamonds."

"Pretty cool, huh?" Jake smiled and began getting the things out of his backpack. He spread one blanket on the ground and the two kids sat down. Jake opened the box of cookies and handed one to Chloe. He got his flashlight out, turned it on and swept it around the trees. "I have to check for wild animals. They're up here you know." He saw Chloe's eyes get big.

"What kind of wild animals?" she asked nervously as she chomped on the cookie.

"All sorts of wild animals. Like bears and mountain lions and sometimes even Bigfoot." He felt even smarter telling her all of this. He knew a lot about the woods.

She frowned. "Bigfoot? Is that for real?"

Jake bit into his cookie. "Of course it is. I've seen him." So he made that up. But he was on a roll. He wanted her to think he was brave too.

"What happened?" she asked excitedly.

"I ran into the woods, right over there." He pointed towards the distance. "And he chased me. But I ran faster than him. And he couldn't catch me." Jake laid down on his back.

Chloe laid down next to him. "That's scary. I hope Bigfoot doesn't come get me."

Jake crossed his hands underneath his head. He wasn't scared. He was brave and he could fight off any old monster. "Don't worry, Chloe. I'll protect you," he responded nonchalantly.

Chloe smiled at him. Then she looked back up at the big sky. "How did you find this place?"

Jake sighed. "After my dad died, my mom quit caring about me. So one night, when she fell asleep, I snuck out and rode and rode and I just found it. It's my secret hiding place."

"You're mommy doesn't love you?" Chloe asked, a look of shock on her little face.

Jake shook his head. "Nope. She says I make her think of Daddy. And she doesn't love Daddy because he didn't love her."

Chloe sat silent for a few seconds, as if she was letting her seven year old brain soak in what Jake was telling her. "Maybe my daddy doesn't love me either. He's always mad at me and tells me to go play. And sometimes, he hits me. It got worse after Mommy died."

Jake turned to her. "What happened to your mommy?"

Chloe stiffened. "I'm not supposed to tell anybody what really happened. That's what Daddy said." She was quiet for a few seconds. And then she spoke up. "But Daddy doesn't love me anymore. So I guess I can tell you." Chloe looked Jake in the eyes. "Daddy said she got so sad that she went crazy. She didn't want to live anymore. One night, I heard my daddy crying in the bathroom. I went in there and saw my mommy in the bathtub." Chloe shuddered at the horrible memory. "There was blood everywhere."

Jake didn't say anything. He wasn't shocked or horrified. He just looked at Chloe. "I hate funerals and cemeteries."

Chloe nodded in agreement. "Me too."

Then Jake shrugged and looked back up at the sky. "But at least my Daddy doesn't come home yelling and hitting me anymore." The two kids laid side by side just staring up at the beautiful sky above them. And then Jake spoke up. "We can't tell anyone about our secret place, ok?"

Chloe nodded again. "Ok." And then she turned to Jake again. "This is a lot of fun, Jake. You're my best friend."

Jake looked at her and smiled back. "You're my best friend, too." And it didn't even matter that she was a girl. To Jake, she was just like him. He pulled the other blanket out of his backpack and draped it over them.

"We're staying out here all night?" she asked, her voice quivering slightly.

"It's like camping. We'll wake up in time to get back home before your dad comes to get you. No one will ever know."

Chloe nervously looked around at the dark, shifting woods that surrounded them. "What if some bear comes and eats us?"

Jake laughed. "I told you, Chloe. I'll protect you!" He giggled until he had her giggling too. "Now go to sleep," he commanded. And she did what he said.

Chapter 8

That fateful night at The Diamond Hills forever sealed Jake & Chloe's friendship. From that moment on, they became inseparable, spending every moment they could with each other, riding bikes all over town, playing ball and sometimes, getting into trouble as kids can do. But mostly, they confided in each other about their abusive, neglectful parents and the trouble they had at home. Even though they were only seven, they both quickly learned that even if they didn't have anything else in this world, they had each other. No one else understood what they were going through. And they didn't dare tell anyone that their parents didn't love them because people came and took kids away from mommies and daddies who didn't love them. They knew *that* by watching T.V. And what would they do if they didn't have each other?

As the summer days passed, Jake and Chloe learned to take care of themselves. Chloe watched carefully as Jake showed her how to make sandwiches and cook macaroni and cheese in the microwave. He taught her how to fix a flat on her bike. She figured out how to work the washer and dryer. She learned what to say when someone called on the telephone asking for her dad who was passed out on the couch with a bottle of whiskey. They learned when to disappear out of sight when people in town started looking at them strangely and wondering why two young kids were all by themselves in the grocery store. Yeah, they were learning a lot. A lot more then what two seven year olds should be learning about. But as long as they had each other, it didn't matter. They were surviving.

One afternoon, Chloe and Jake were playing baseball in a nearby park. Jake smacked the ball way out into left field. The ball soared over some bushes and landed near the back yards of some houses. Chloe quickly ran to retrieve it. She got down on her hands and knees and crawled through the underbrush until she spotted it lying near a fence. As she crept closer, she heard laughter coming from the backyard of one of the houses. Chloe peered through the fence. Somebody was having a birthday party. The backyard was decorated with colorful streamers and balloons. She saw a table filled to the brim with presents. Another table had a huge white and pink cake on it and a big glass bowl filled with red punch. A group of girls held hands and danced around in a circle chanting "Ring Around the Rosie." They all had ribbons in their hair and wore pretty dresses full of ruffles. They giggled and smiled and seemed so happy. These little girls were so pretty. Chloe glanced down at her scabbed over knees and legs full of scratches and bruises. Her shorts had a tear in them and her shoes were scuffed up and dirty. She didn't look anything like them.

Just then, a woman came out of the house and asked if the girls were having fun. They all ran over to her telling her yes. The woman wrapped her arms around one little girl and gave her a big kiss on the cheek. "I love you, darling. Happy Birthday!"

The little girl kissed her mother back and told her, "I love you too, Mommy. Thank you for such a wonderful party!"

The woman spoke to all of the girls. "Now as soon as Jennifer's daddy gets here, he's going to take all of you to the zoo!" The girls all squealed with delight and clapped their hands.

"Can we open presents now, Mommy!" asked the birthday girl.

"Sure can. Come on girls!"

Chloe wasn't sure how long she hid in the bushes watching it all. But tears began welling up in her eyes. God she wished she had a mommy and daddy like that. Even when her mom was alive, she never hugged and kissed her. She just laid in bed and cried. And Daddy was always so mad…Chloe wiped another tear that fell from her eyes.

"What are you doing!" came Jake's frantic whisper from behind her.

Chloe jumped. He had come to see where she had disappeared to.

He frowned when he saw the tears. "Why are you crying?" he asked, trying to be quiet.

Chloe pointed towards the yard where the girls were giggling and opening up presents filled with dolls and dishes. "I just wish I could have all that."

Jake looked towards the girls. "Why? They're just a bunch of stupid girls playing with stupid dolls. You don't even like that stuff."

Chloe sniffled and pointed to the lady who was smiling down at her daughter. "Maybe I would like them if I had a mommy like that. That mommy loves her kid!" And Chloe cried harder.

"Shhh!" warned Jake. "Come on! Let's get out here before they hear us!" He grabbed the ball and then tugged on her arm. She followed him until they were in the clear.

Chloe continued to cry softly. Jake didn't say anything. The two just slowly walked back towards the park. Chloe walked up to a bench and sat down, sobbing.

Jake sat down next to her. He put his arm around her shoulder. "Don't cry, Chloe. It'll be alright."

Chloe sniffled and wiped the snot from her nose with the back of her dirty hand. "When I grow up, I'm *never* going to be mean to my kids! I'm going to love them and hug them and throw them birthday parties and take them to the zoo. And I'm *never* going to leave them like my mommy left me!"

Jake just sat there, listening to her sob. And then he spoke up. "Please stop crying, Chloe. You know it makes me sad when you cry. And it makes me want to cry too." He looked down at the ground. "I'm the boy. I'm supposed to be brave." But his voice began to shake. And then he sighed and looked back up at her. "I know your mommy left you. But I won't leave you."

Chloe looked at him with watery, red eyes. "You won't?"

He shook his head. "Nope."

"You promise!" she sniffled.

He smiled at her. "I promise." He stood up then. "Come on. We better get back."

Chloe rubbed her eyes and stood up too. They picked up their bat and ball, kicking pebbles on the ground as they slowly made their way home.

Chapter 9

Gloria Smith had been a second grade teacher for ten years now at Johnson Elementary. But in all those ten years, she had never seen what she had witnessed today. Then again, it was very rare to have students in her class along the likes of Jake Stevens and Chloe Mayer. They were disadvantaged kids growing up in very troubled, abusive homes. She knew that. But what she didn't expect was the bond these two kids shared and how intensely they watched out for each other.

It was three weeks into the new school year and while all the other little kids were outside playing, here little Jake and Chloe sat at their desks during recess, in trouble, *yet again*. Jake was developing a black eye. And a big purple bruise was forming on Chloe's left cheek. Gloria stared sternly at the two kids who refused to look up at her.

She had witnessed it all on the playground. Timmy Robbins was teasing Chloe about her "crazy, dead mother" as he put it. Before Gloria could make it over to the kids, Chloe had shoved Timmy, who then proceeded to punch Chloe in the face. The next thing she knew, Jake had jumped on top of Timmy, punching him and yelling at the top of his lungs, "Leave her alone! Don't you ever touch her again!"

Sure, kids stuck up for one another on the playground but she had never seen so much fury come out of one little boy who fought so fearlessly to defend his friend in need. It was as if he knew he had to protect her from all the bad things this world was dishing out at them.

Gloria sighed. "You know, the school nurse is doctoring up Timmy Robbins' busted lip as we speak." She waited for a response. Silence. Gloria glared at Jake and Chloe. "Tell me why I shouldn't march you two up to the principal's office right now for some well deserved swats and three days' suspension from school!" Still nothing. She leaned back into her chair and crossed her arms in front of her chest. "Well, fighting is against school rules and you two seemed to have gotten into quite a few scuffles the last several weeks," she stated plainly. The two kids seemed bound and determined not to break their code of silence. Gloria turned to Chloe, the little tomboy of a girl with the saddest eyes she had ever seen. "I'm going to have to call your dad, Chloe."

Without looking up, Chloe muttered, "Go ahead. He won't answer the phone."

"And why not?"

"Because he drinks and then falls asleep on the couch." The little girl's tone was so matter-of-fact.

Gloria gulped hard, realizing that the every day occurrence of Bill Mayer's inebriation had already numbed this lost little girl sitting in front of her. Gloria tried to hide the sickness she felt creeping into her gut. She figured Jake's situation wasn't any different. These kids had seen and experienced things that no seven year old kid should have to see or experience. And they knew just as well as she did how things worked. Jake and Chloe were just two more statistics of a failed system where kids fell through the cracks. It happened all the time. Whether it was because of fear or denial, it was just easier for people to look the other way or not acknowledge it at all.

Gloria's hands were tied. There was not a damned thing she could do. These kids were, basically, on their own. Sadly, they had already figured that out. No one was going to help them. They only had each other to cling to.

Gloria did the only thing she could do. She sat forward and looked them both dead on. "Look at me, both of you. Right now."

Jake and Chloe slowly raised their hollow eyes to hers.

She spoke slowly and clearly, hoping that if they got one thing out of all the things she would teach them throughout the year, *this* would be it. "The only way you're going to get out of this…to rise above this…is to quit getting into trouble. *Please* stay away from all the bad things you're seeing and that you're going to see. Stay in school and study hard. Work hard. Make good grades. That's your ticket. That's your only way out of all this." She paused as Jake and Chloe blinked silently back at her with identical brown eyes. "I know it might not all make sense right now. But trust me on this. Do you understand?"

The two kids nodded their heads. And she knew they really did understand. They understood a whole lot more than the average seven year old did or should for that matter. She pointed a finger at them, her eyes narrowing. "Most importantly, don't ever, ever forget what you two have." She leaned back against her chair again. "It's the only thing that's getting you through."

Jake and Chloe looked at each other and then back at Gloria.

Gloria rubbed her forehead. "I'm not going to send you to Mr. Blackwell's office. You can go." The kids looked shocked and then relieved. They quickly got up and left the classroom.

Gloria stared out her window and spotted Jake and Chloe running out of the school building and towards the merry-go-round. She shook her head, knowing she was going to have hell to pay, especially when Timmy Robbins' parents came hollering. But she would find a way to deal with it. Chloe and Jake needed someone to believe in them. So she prayed for them silently as she sat at her desk and wiped the tears that formed in the corner of her eyes. And she hoped to hell they would remember what she had just told them. It was their only chance.

Ten Years Later…

Chapter 10

Molly Watters bounded out her front door and practically ran down her drive towards the black 4X4 extended cab pickup that sat waiting for her at the curb. She stopped at the passenger side window, looking in and smiling from ear to ear. "Hi," she breathlessly replied, trying hard to control her excitement.

He gave her a killer smile. "Hey," his deep, sexy voice responded.

She quickly opened the door and climbed into the truck. Turning towards him, she transfixed her eyes upon his clean cut dark hair, intense brown eyes and strong jaw. He wore a black leather jacket, blue jeans and biker boots – the epitome of the bad boy image. He was tall, dark and handsome. No…better yet…he was hot. *Extremely hot*. And she was in his truck, sitting right beside him. Could things get any better?

"You ready?" he asked, his voice low and steady. He gave her another intense smile that sent shivers down her spine.

She smiled back. "Yeah…I am," she replied, trying hard to steady her own voice.

Molly watched as Jake Stevens turned up the radio which blasted hard rock music filled with electric guitar riffs and a pounding base line. He shifted the truck into gear and sped out into the night. She felt her heart skip a beat when he reached over and grabbed her hand. His fingers intertwined with hers. God, her stomach was filled with butterflies. Moving to this town and transferring to a new high school was turning out to be a real blessing.

As they turned onto the main drag, Molly quickly stole another glance at Jake. He had captivated her from the moment she laid eyes on him. At six feet tall with a strong, athletic build, he was breathtakingly good looking. She remembered catching a glimpse of him this past summer at the public pool and nearly fell over when she saw his rock hard, six pack abs, built chest and strong arms. He was simply the most beautiful guy she had ever seen. But what also captivated her was his multifaceted personality. The girls at school had told her he was mysterious, kind, smart and a rebel all rolled into one. Jake was a true enigma, impossible to figure out. But Molly planned to be the girl that would peel back the layers, one by one.

Jake squeezed her hand, making her smile again. "You look really nice tonight, Molly," Jake told her.

She instantly blushed, looking away for a split second at the cars they were passing. "Thank you," she replied. "You do too."

They began making small talk, easing into their first date. As they drove, Jake listened intently while Molly spoke of her classes and the teachers she had and how excited she was to be a senior. He simply grinned at her comments, making her heart skip another beat.

The anticipation of what Jake had planned for the evening was killing Molly. She finally had to ask him. "So where are we going?" She smiled, taking him all in again, trying her best to slow her breathing down.

He looked at her from the corner of his eyes. "You'll see…" He grinned, exciting her even more and proving true to the fact that he *was* mysterious. "But first…I have to make a pit stop."

Molly said nothing as Jake turned off the main drag and began heading down some residential streets that led to a rougher, poorer looking neighborhood. She looked out her window at the houses and yards that were the complete opposite of the houses and yards in her own upscale neighborhood. These homes displayed peeling paint and weed ridden lawns. Old cars and trucks sat parked on cracked driveways. Unsure of what he had planned or why they were in this part of town, Molly quickly asked, "Are we picking somebody up?"

"Yep," was all Jake said. He came to a stop in front of an old two story house.

She stared at the tiny yard and the sagging front porch. And then she turned back to Jake. "Who?" she asked, puzzled.

A huge smile spread across Jake's lips and his eyes seemed to sparkle. "My best friend." He nodded his head towards the passenger window as his eyes reverted back to the house.

Molly slowly turned and looked out the window. She saw a girl come out the front door carrying a bottle of beer in her right hand. Tall and slender, she wore baggy canvas pants, biker boots and an old army jacket. Her long brown hair was pulled casually back into a ponytail. She looked tough, like she could kick anyone's ass if they got in her way.

The girl opened the passenger door and got in. Without cracking a smile, she looked Molly up and down. "You must be Molly. I'm Chloe." She extended her hand towards Molly.

Completely shell shocked, Molly nervously shook Chloe's hand and offered a shaky hello. Chloe didn't reciprocate the greeting. She just turned forward and took a slug of beer as Jake put the pickup in gear and took off towards the main streets of town.

As they drove, Molly remained silent, unsure what to say next. She sat between Jake and Chloe wondering how in the world the two of them ever became best friends. Jake must have sensed her nervousness because he took her hand into his again. Molly turned and looked at Chloe who seemed miles away as she looked straight ahead. "So...how long have you two known each other?" she asked in a futile attempt to make conversation.

Chloe took another slug of her beer and looked at her. "Since we were 7." And then she turned forward again.

"Wow, you guys grew up together." The instant it came out, Molly cringed, realizing she had just stated the obvious.

Chloe grunted under her breath. "You got it."

If that was Chloe's attempt at making Molly feel stupid, it worked. She didn't notice Jake crack a small grin over it all. But what she did notice was Chloe…and how stunningly pretty she was even though she wore no makeup. Her long, dark lashes made her brown eyes stand out against her skin which was just like porcelain. Her lips were full and had a natural tint of red to them. She was mesmerizing.

Molly decided to take another stab at making conversation. "So…where are *you* heading tonight, Chloe?"

Chloe turned towards her. "Don't worry, Molly." And then she grinned, "I'm not gonna tag along on your date."

Molly tried to smile and play it cool. But for some reason, Chloe was doing a good job at making Molly feel like a complete idiot.

Chloe looked up ahead and pointed. "Hey, floor it!"

Jake sped up until they came along side another pickup truck. Molly could see two guys in it. The driver had light brown hair and the passenger was blonde. Both young men were blessed with good looks as well. When the two guys inside caught sight of them, they whooped and hollered like a bunch of drunk assholes. And then Molly saw them both slug back beers. Ok, forget *like*. They *were* drunk assholes. Chloe grinned. Jake hollered back at them. Molly quickly figured out that they all knew each other. Once again, she felt out of place.

Jake began speeding up, racing along side the other pickup. Molly felt her heart pounding. What the hell was going on?

Chloe shouted out the window. "Where's my beer, Brad! I won fair and square! And Jeff, you owe me too! I saw you cheating!"

Brad laughed out loud like a crazy person as he gripped the steering wheel tighter. "You want it? You come get it!" He pressed his foot on the gas and sped up even faster.

Chloe burst out laughing and Jake grinned as he sped up too. Molly squeezed Jake's arm and watched as the speedometer needle shot up to 95 mph. She felt the wind whipping all around her in the cab of the pickup and the engine roaring in her ears. This was crazy!

Jake was neck and neck with the other vehicle as they barreled down the street, careening around cars that seemed to be sitting still. Carefully, Jake eased over closer to his right. Chloe began sticking her legs out the window.

Molly's eyes grew to the size of lemons. "What are you doing!?" she exclaimed.

Chloe looked over her shoulder at Molly with a crazy look in her eyes, as if she was high on drugs. "Catchin' a ride," a smart-ass tone to her voice.

Molly grabbed Chloe by the arm, an instinct reaction perhaps. "Well, what's wrong with pulling over?!"

Chloe casually handed Molly her beer. She grinned. "Now, come on, Molly! Where's the fun in that?"

And Molly watched with horror as Chloe, in one swift move, lifted her hips and swung her body up and out of the pickup. She methodically turned herself around, hanging on through the open window, standing along the running board, her hair getting whipped wildly around by the speed at which they were traveling. Brad and Jeff were hollering and cheering her on at the top of their lungs. Molly looked at the speedometer again. 100 mph. God, Chloe was going to kill herself! They were all going to die! She turned to Jake. He was grinning from ear to ear, alternating between watching Chloe and watching the road, driving like a crazy man.

Suddenly, Molly saw Chloe let go and jump across towards the other pickup. She hung on to side of the bed as Jake and the other guys hollered in approval. Chloe swiftly moved towards the door of the pickup, strong and steady. Like some sort of circus acrobat, she somehow managed to sit on the sill of the open window, grabbing onto the side mirror as an anchor. And then Molly watched Chloe bend her body and duck her head to slide into the pickup. Brad slid over as Chloe took over the wheel. Jake laughed and howled like a wolf. Molly thought she was going to puke. She held her hand over her heart, trying her best to catch her breath. Jesus Christ! They were all completely insane!

Chloe draped her left arm out the window and casually smiled at Molly again. "Nice meeting you, Molly." Her voice was calm and unwavering.

Molly was too busy trying to recover from what had just happened that she failed to notice Jake and Chloe stealing a glance at each other, saying something with their eyes that no one else could read. A bond that only the two of them shared. Chloe looked at Molly again and gave her one last crazy grin. She sped up, took the next turn and quickly disappeared out of sight.

Jake slowed the pickup down back to a legal speed limit. He laughed to himself and turned to Molly. "You alright?" he asked, squeezing her hand.

Molly slowed her breathing down. "Yeah, I'm ok. God, that was nuts." Her hand shook as she ran it through her long, blonde hair.

Jake laughed again.

Molly looked at him. "That Chloe, she's something else, isn't she?"

Jake kept his eyes on the road and grinned. "Yeah….she sure is."

Chapter 11

The black sky was perfectly clear. Not a cloud in sight. Chloe arched her neck and looked up at the stars. They were beautiful tonight. A slight nip in the air reminded her that autumn was just around the corner. And the tall trees of the vast forest that surrounded her danced lazily in a gentle breeze. Chloe stood with her friends, Brad Wilson & Jeff Allen, taking in the huge, outdoor rave that was transpiring all around them. Several bonfires were blazing and a DJ blasted edgy music from huge speakers. As far as the eye could see, teenagers were dancing, mingling, laughing and drinking. It was definitely the party to be at.

"God, I need to get laid tonight," replied Jeff, taking a swig from his beer and stealing a glance at a pretty girl who was strolling by. The breeze tousled his dirty blond hair, making a few strands fall over his forehead.

Chloe rolled her eyes. "Didn't you just get laid last night? What was her name…Sherry, Carrie…Mary?"

Brad laughed. "You expect him to know her name?"

Chloe grinned. "Yeah, what was I thinking?"

Jeff draped his arms around his two buddies' shoulders. "Now come on, you're making me out to be some worthless prick. I have feelings you know."

Chloe laughed. "Yeah, unfortunately, they're all emanating from below your waistline."

Brad burst out laughing, holding onto his side. Jeff just shook his head, taking the blow like a trooper. The three friends continued to harmlessly taunt and tease each other, all the while having a good time and enjoying each other's company.

A guy, blonde and handsome, walked by just then, trying to be discreet as he eyed Chloe. Chloe looked over at him and he smiled at her. She smiled back. He moved along, disappearing into the crowds, apparently not ready to make a move.

"Don't even think about it," responded Brad, witnessing the whole interchange. His hazel green eyes flashed Chloe a look of warning.

Chloe frowned. "Why not?"

"Because he's just as bad as Jeff. I've seen him in action."

Jeff stepped up. "Yeah, he's a jerk."

Chloe caught sight of the blonde haired, blue eyed guy again. He was stealing glances at her.

Brad spoke up, shifting Chloe's focus back to her friends. "You know Jake will end up kicking his ass."

Chloe looked at her friends and frowned. "I can take care of myself." And she could. She was tough as nails. Everyone knew it.

Jeff grunted. "Tell that to Jake." He moved the bottle of beer up to his lips and took another slug.

Chloe remained silent, slowly sipping her own beer. After a bit, she casually looked over at the guy again who was still smiling at her. She smiled and shyly looked away.

Chapter 12

Jake and Molly walked out of the restaurant and got back into the pickup. They headed down the open road. Molly slid her body close to his and he wrapped his arm around her. She felt the butterflies again. "That was a really nice place, Jake. Thank you."

"I'm glad you liked it." He began playing gently with her hair, twirling the golden locks with his fingers.

Molly looked at his handsome face, secretly studying his profile. "So…what now?"

He grinned. "You feel like going to a party?"

She piped up. "A party? Where at?"

He rubbed her shoulder. "Ever been to the 'The Diamond Hills'?"

Molly shook her head no. "I've never heard of it. What's it like?"

Jake grinned again. "You'll see." Once again, his answer was clouded in mystery. Molly shivered with anticipation as Jake turned up the radio and sped towards the winding road that led deep into the woods.

After weaving back and forth on hairpin curves and climbing steep inclines, they finally pulled up to the rave that seemed to be in full swing. At least two hundred teenagers blanketed the area, taking refuge within the seclusion of the forest. Molly stared at the huge bonfires that lit up the night sky and all of the surrounding chaos. "Wow, this is great!" exclaimed Molly.

She and Jake got out and began walking towards the party. They began meeting up with people they knew. Molly scanned the whole scene and felt exhilarated. She had never seen anything like this. Everyone seemed so carefree and uninhibited. It made her want to be uninhibited too.

Molly watched as girls tried to catch Jake's eye as they passed. He was a chick magnet as lame as that sounded. But it was true. They gawked at him, smiled at him and tried to make small talk, not caring that Molly was standing right beside him. But it didn't bother her. In fact, it made her feel good that she was the one on his arm.

Molly's girlfriends finally caught up to her, eager to talk about all the people that were here.

"I'm going to grab a beer. You want one?" Jake asked Molly. Nodding yes, she and all of her friends watched him walk away.

"Man, Molly. He is sooo hot! How are things going with him?" asked Susan, one of her friends.

Molly grinned. "So far, so good. He's very nice." She was trying to keep her enthusiasm for Jake as low key as possible. But she knew her friends were seeing right through her. They teased her, making her blush.

In the midst of joking and chatting with her girlfriends, Molly spotted Chloe with Jeff and Brad, the two guys she crazily jumped into the speeding pickup with. She tugged Susan on the arm. "Hey, tell me something. What's *her* story?" She nodded towards Chloe.

Susan quickly figured out who Molly was trying to point out. "Who, Chloe Mayer? Interesting girl, huh?" Susan leaned in, talking low. "From what I hear, she had a messed up childhood growing up, just like Jake. I guess that's why they bonded."

Molly nodded. Her friends had already filled her in about Jake's abusive, broken upbringing. She and Susan continued to eye Chloe.

And then Susan leaned in again. "Her mother went nuts and killed herself by slitting her wrists in the bathtub. Little seven-year-old Chloe saw it all."

Molly couldn't tear her eyes away from Chloe. "My God. That's awful."

Susan nodded in agreement. "And her dad's not any better. He's a raging alcoholic."

Molly continued to listen, all the while watching Chloe from a distance, who just stood alongside her friends, observing the crowds.

"She's keeps to herself a lot. Unless you mess with her."

Molly spoke up. "She looks so lost. But she's beautiful."

Susan sighed. "Yep, none of them will admit it, but every guy here is dying to see what's underneath all that baggy clothes."

Molly looked at Susan. "You're serious?"

Susan laughed. "I guess it keeps them guessing." She paused for a second. "But Jake won't let that happen."

Molly frowned. "What do you mean?"

Susan shook her head as if she was trying to understand it herself. "They're tight. He watches out for her. And from what I hear, he always has."

Their conversation was interrupted when more people came up and began talking to them. Jake returned then with two beers. He handed one to Molly and smiled at her. She suddenly forgot all about Chloe and focused on those intense, deep brown eyes that were looking right into hers.

Chapter 13

He was walking up to her, smiling. So what if he was a male slut? Chloe was a big girl. She could handle it. And she certainly wasn't going to run. Besides, she was all alone now, sitting by herself on the tailgate of somebody's pickup. Brad and Jeff had long since abandoned her as they stood a few feet away talking with some girls. She needed someone to talk to too.

"Hi, Chloe," he said.

She was shocked that he knew her name. Chloe wasn't exactly popular at the huge high school she attended. "Hi," she timidly replied.

"I'm Ty."

"Nice to meet you, Ty," she politely told him. It was funny. When it came to guys, her tough girl persona faded and she felt herself softening and becoming more feminine.

Ty nervously looked at Brad & Jeff who had noticed he had come up. He must have felt their guard being raised and the sudden tension in the air. Ty leaned in and whispered, "Do you wanna go somewhere and talk?"

Chloe stole a glance at her buddies. Yep, they were giving her that knowing look, warning her about him. Chloe looked at Ty. He was good looking, with golden blonde hair and intense blue eyes. It was impossible not to feel an instant attraction towards him, even if he didn't have the best of reputations. The mere fact that he was even interested in her was flattering. Warning bells were sounding all around her, from in her head and from her friends. *Oh, what the hell!* Tonight, she was going to ignore them. Chloe smiled. "Sure…let's go."

Ty grinned.

Chloe jumped down from the tailgate of the pickup she was sitting on and winced slightly from the pain that shot up from her right hip. She grinned and bared it, following Ty as he began walking away, nervously hoping that he had not noticed. He didn't.

Chapter 14

But Jake saw it all. And he knew it wasn't because of her stunt with the pickup from earlier this evening. "Damn it!" he mumbled under his breath.

"What did you say?" asked Molly who was busy chatting with her friends.

"Nothing," he replied and tried to be discreet as he watched Chloe leaving with the guy. *It had happened again.* Jake felt his blood begin to boil. But he had to keep his cool. There was no need to cause a scene now. He'd deal with it later.

"Hey, wanna go somewhere quieter?" Molly asked as she circled her arms around Jake's waist. He turned his attention back to her. She was giving him that look. A look he had seen countless times. Jake smiled. It always came so easily for him. He never had to beg. And she was very pretty, with long blonde hair and big blue eyes.

There had been so many. She was about to become another one. He just couldn't help it. He kissed her hard on the lips.

"Let's go." His voice was filled with lust. He took her hand and led her away from the party, back to his pickup. Once inside, they wasted no time in ravishing each other. She tore her clothes off and sat on top of him. Jake gave her what she wanted, touching her in all the right places, pushing himself deep inside of her, making her scream with pleasure. He closed his eyes and let himself go. And when they were done, she collapsed against him. Neither of them moved.

Molly lifted her head and looked him in the eyes. "That was amazing." And then she blushed. "I usually don't do this on a first date. There's just something about you." She gave him a sensuous kiss and laid her head down on his chest, holding him tightly. "Oh, Jake. I could stay like this forever."

Jake closed his eyes again. Why did she have to say that? In the heat of passion, he had given her what she wanted, but he wouldn't be able to give her what she was wanting now. Just like all the rest, she'd figure that out. Jake kept his eyes closed, thankful that it was dark in his pickup and Molly couldn't see his face. He kissed the top of her head and circled his arms around her too.

Chapter 15

Ty Snyder looked at Chloe, trying to figure her out. She was mysterious in so many ways. They had been chatting for awhile. He could tell she was loosening up a bit, smiling as she talked, laughing at his funny comments. Yet, she was still edgy and nervous, holding herself back. He knew this was going to take some work. "So what do you do for fun?" he asked. "Besides go to crazy raves at 'The Hills'?"

Chloe looked down and grinned. "I stay pretty busy with my job. I'm a waitress at Neveah's."

Ty raised an eyebrow. "Neveah's! Wow, that's a five star restaurant." He took a drink from his cup.

"Yeah, it's a good job. The tips are great. The patrons are mostly rich businessmen and their mistresses of course."

Ty laughed. "I bet you see a lot!"

Chloe giggled. "Oh, too much! You'd be amazed at what I've seen."

He didn't expect her to be so easy to talk to. She was kind and smart and damn, the more he looked at her, the prettier she got. He wanted to make a move. Would she let him?

Ty moved in cautiously and kissed her. She began kissing him back, slowly. He touched her cheek and heard her breathing quicken. He became instantly aroused. But he knew he had better take it slow if he wanted any chance with her. Ty reluctantly pulled away, surprised at how fast his heart was racing. She seemed excited too. "I guess we better get back," he replied. He took her hand and led her back to the party.

"There you are!" someone called from behind them. Ty and Chloe turned around to see some girls walking up.

"Hey Samantha! Where have you been?" asked Chloe.

"Right here! This place is crazy! It's hard to find anyone," replied Samantha. She and the other girls looked at Ty.

Chloe quickly introduced him to everyone. "Oh, Ty, these are my friends, Samantha, Tracy, Brooke and Jenny." The girls grinned at him, telling him hello. He exchanged greetings with them as well.

"So tell me, where is Jake tonight?" asked Tracy, her eyes sparkling. It was obvious to Ty that she was absolutely head over heels for Jake.

Chloe looked around. "He *was* here. Hmmm, I don't know. Must have disappeared somewhere."

Tracy looked disappointed. "Shoot! I've finally mustered up the courage to go up and talk to him."

Chloe grunted. "Better take a number."

Ty smiled at her wise crack. She was very witty. He wanted to spend more time with her alone. But it was apparent that her girlfriends were interested in hanging out for a while. And so he patiently stood by her side, listening to their conversations and politely responding to their questions. Before long, Chloe reached for his hand and led him a few feet away. Ty's heart started to pound again.

She looked up at him. "I think I'm going to call it a night."

He was disappointed. "Already? It's early yet."

She looked down at the ground. "I'm a little tired." Lifting her head again, she smiled at him. "I really enjoyed talking with you tonight."

Ty squeezed her hand. "I did too. Maybe we can do it again sometime."

"Yeah, that would be nice."

Ty looked over at Brad and Jeff. The two Casanovas were busy making out with some girls. He smirked. "I have a feeling they're going to be tied up for a while. You want me to take you home?"

Chloe glanced over at her male friends. She laughed, shaking her head. "Thanks, but I'll get a ride with Samantha. We need to catch up on all our girl talk." She winked at him.

He laughed, still wishing she could stay. And then he grew serious, moving in close and kissing her tenderly on the lips. They told each other goodbye. He watched as she walked back towards her girlfriends. Chloe bid the others goodbye and left with Samantha.

Chapter 16

It was late by the time Jake had dropped Molly off and pulled into his drive. His house was pitch black inside. She was gone again. No telling where she was or what she was doing. His mom had really spiraled downward the last several years. Her escalating addiction to alcohol and drugs had totally consumed her. She had never mentally been around for him through the years, but now, she physically wasn't around. Jake had no idea if she would come home or not. Sometimes it was days. His mom had hated his dad for what he did to them. But here she was acting just like him. One day, if she didn't slow down, Jake would find her dead. He rubbed his eyes. It just didn't seem to get any easier.

Jake looked down the street towards Chloe's house and saw her shadow walking across her bedroom window. She was still awake. He jogged over and began climbing the lattice that led to her open window. Just as he looked in, he saw her pull up her pajama pants up over her hip. She had been looking at something.

Chloe froze and locked eyes with Jake. He climbed in. She reached for her lamp and turned off the light. Darkness enveloped them. Jake stood there until his eyes adjusted. She looked away. He knew she was ashamed, wanting to hide what he had just seen. She crawled on top of her bed and laid down, turning away from him.

Jake took his jacket off and sat down beside her. He reached out and touched her hip gently. Her hand bolted to his to stop him. "Let me see," he whispered.

She let go and he could see her watching him in the dark. Moving ever so slowly, Jake gently lifted her t-shirt with one hand and with the other, pulled her pajama pants down just enough to reveal her bare hip. Even in the darkness, he could see the red gash that had begun to scab over. A big purple bruise surrounded it. Jake grazed the wound with his fingertips, feeling Chloe begin to tremble underneath them. God, it hurt him so badly to see her like this. She had no idea how much it enraged him.

And then his eyes traveled to the smooth, soft skin that extended from her hip to her small waist all the way around to her flat, toned stomach. He felt his pulse quickening as excitement began replacing his anger and rage. His fingertips left the wound and slowly moved up her hip. His eyes shot up to hers. In the moonlit room, he could see that look in her eyes again. The look that begged him to stop but also begged him to keep going too. It was another moment. Another moment that scared them to death just as much as the first time it happened. He closed his eyes, remembering it like yesterday.

Jake could feel his mind screaming inside, making him crazy. Holding himself back was getting harder and harder each time. He opened his eyes to see Chloe silently crying. Was it from the physical pain she was experiencing? Or was she tormented too, confused and terrified about what was happening between them? Jake laid down with her, pulling her close to him. She took his hand in hers and held on tightly. He breathed in the sweet scent of her hair and felt her soft, warm curves next to his body. Chloe trembled as Jake closed his eyes again and kissed the back of her head. He felt himself melting into her. She made him feel like they were the only two people left in this dark world. He whispered into her ear, "I wish we could just disappear, Chloe. Disappear so that no one could ever find us. So that no one could ever hurt you again." Chloe softly kissed his hand that she held and he felt a million bolts of electricity shoot up his arm and through his body. He lay there a long time in the dark, listening to her breathing until it steadied and he knew she had fallen asleep. Jake closed his eyes, held her even tighter and succumbed to the darkness.

Chapter 17

The sobbing reverberated throughout the whole house. It made her ears hurt so much that she had to cover them with her hands. Where the hell was it coming from? She had to make it stop.

She opened her bedroom door and stepped into the dark hallway. The sobbing was deafening now. "Daddy? Is that you?" she called. She started down the hallway but the floor grew longer and the walls stretched. She was walking and then running but getting nowhere. "Daddy!" she screamed. "Daddy, what's wrong?" In an all out sprint she tried to make it to the bathroom door that was opened just a crack. An eerie glow illuminated from it.

Suddenly, she fell flat on her face. When she lifted her head, she saw that she was lying in front of the door. The sobbing had died down to a soft whimper. She stood up and inched the door slowly open. Her dad was kneeling at the edge of the bathtub, hunched over with his head in his hands, crying. It seemed a million candles were burning throughout the whole room. She walked slowly towards the bathtub until her mother came into full view. She was pale as a ghost, her eyes closed, her hair sopping wet. Her right arm hung over the side of the tub. And that's when she saw the drops of blood on the floor. They dripped from her wrists in perfect time, like a leaky faucet. The water in the tub was blood red. Her beautiful mother lay dead and limp, like a rag doll. She felt her stomach start to turn. So much so that she had to cover her mouth and gag several times. But she couldn't tear her eyes away from her mother. She was gone. Gone forever. Suddenly, her mother's eyes popped open with an evil stare and her bloody arm bolted out to grab her in the face. And she began to scream…

Chloe sat straight up in bed, scared to death. She looked around, terrified of what she might see. She tried to catch her breath, holding her hand over her chest. She laid back down and stared up at the ceiling, realizing it was just a another nightmare, one of many she's had since she was a kid. God, they were becoming more realistic each time.

Her clock read 2:43 am. She closed her eyes to try and go back to sleep when she heard distant shouting coming from outside her open window. Chloe got up and looked out. In the moonlight, she could see two dark figures standing on Jake's lawn. Jesus Christ. It was Clarissa.

Chloe quickly got dressed and headed downstairs. As she ran up to the two of them, she could see that Clarissa was severely intoxicated and strung out.

"Mom, just get in the house!" shouted Jake. "You're going to wake everyone up!" He reached out for her.

Clarissa shoved her son off. "Who gives a shit! Do you think anyone around here gives a shit about me?!"

"You're drunk, Mom! You need to sleep this off!"

Chloe could see the anguish in Jake's face.

Clarissa stumbled around. "You don't know what I need! Nobody knows what I need! Not you! Not your dead father! Not anyone!" She was screaming now at the top of her lungs, incomprehensible gibberish spewing out from her drunken lips.

Suddenly she stopped and fell to her knees. Jake lunged for her. Her body heaved and she began to vomit in the grass. Wretched noises bellowed from deep within her as the vile stuff came up in buckets. Jake held his mom, trying to keep her from collapsing.

THE DIAMOND HILLS

Chloe stood there, covering her mouth, witnessing the horror and not knowing what to do.

Chloe thought it would never end. It seemed Jake's mother was puking all of her guts out. Finally, Clarissa slumped against Jake's shoulder, completely lifeless. Chloe ran over to them and helped Jake pull his mother up to her feet. The smell was horrible. They clumsily dragged her into the house and to her bedroom. Chloe watched as Jake carefully laid his mother on the bed and covered her up with a blanket. He tenderly wiped the remnant vomit from her chin with a Kleenex. Clarissa might as well have been dead. She was white as a sheet with sunken in eyes and hollow cheeks. Her hair was ratty and dirty. She looked 80 years old. But Clarissa Stevens…was only 43.

Jake closed his mother's bedroom door and followed Chloe out to the living room. He sat down on the couch and put his face in his hands. Chloe sat down next to him, feeling his pain. "She's going to die. She's going to die," he whimpered. He began sobbing, his shoulders heaving up and down.

Chloe rubbed his back, trying her best to comfort her best friend. She cried too. She had never been as brave as Jake. And so fearfully, she cried too.

Chapter 18

Brad, Jeff and Jake cruised down the street in Jake's pickup, drinking like fish and blasting the radio. It was another Saturday night out on the town and the boys were feeling wild. Jeff slugged his beer back, reached outside the window and flung his empty bottle into the back of Jake's pickup bed. "I hear Molly's going to be at 'The Hills' tonight," he slurred. He leaned forward and rested his arm on the back of Jake's seat.

Jake ran his fingers through his hair. "Shit, we're not going there then."

Brad laughed. "You're a dog."

"Screw you! You're a dog too," retaliated Jake. He was not in a good mood. He was tired from working all day at his job with the highway road construction crew. Jake always put in long hours after school and on the weekends. It was hard work but it paid good, and these days, Jake needed all the money he could get to help pay the bills. His mom was quite frankly, becoming worthless. She had gotten fired from her last two jobs. And Jake figured she wouldn't last very long at the one she was at now. It was a sore subject between the two of them. In fact, just before he had left tonight, she had given him hell, fighting with him again.

Jeff spoke up, referring to Molly again. "Well how long did this one last? A month? Two?"

Brad joked. "Wow, a new record." He looked out his window at the passing scenery.

Jake looked straight ahead, not cracking a smile at his friends' smart-ass remarks. "She'll get over it. Just like they all do."

Brad whistled low. "I would have tapped that ass a little longer. She was hot, man."

Jake took a swig of his beer. "Yeah, I guess she was."

Jeff sat back and put his hands behind his head. "So where's Chloe tonight?"

Jake grunted. "Out with that prick again." He was talking about Ty Snyder.

Jeff laughed. "You say that about all the guys she likes."

"Well he is."

"You think they're getting serious?" asked Brad. "She's been spending an awful lot of time with him."

Jake didn't take his eyes from the road. "Who knows? Who cares? He's just another horny bastard who just wants to get laid."

Laughing, Jeff stated the obvious. "Well, we're just a bunch of horny bastards who just want to get laid and Chloe hangs out with us."

Jake shook his head. "That's different and you know it."

Brad and Jeff grew silent. Jake knew then that they were picking up on his agitation. And then Brad turned to Jake. "You know, you can't protect her forever."

Jake looked at his friend, soaking in the words that just came out of his mouth. He turned back to the road, slammed the rest of his beer and threw the bottle out the window onto the street. The glass shattered into a million pieces.

Sirens sounded behind them. Blue and red lights flashed in Jake's rearview mirror. Brad and Jeff turned around. "You better pull over, man," stated Brad.

But Jake was in a bad mood. And he wanted to get into a good mood…fast! "Nope, not tonight boys!" He accelerated as his buddies howled and cheered him on. Hot damn! The chase was on! And Jake wasn't about to get caught.

They led the cops through a maze of side streets and back alleys. Skidding off the main road, they headed in the direction of the woods. Jake would lose them there. He always did. The police siren blared into the night, so loud it could have awakened the dead. Jake grinned and pushed his foot all the way down on the accelerator. "Hold on, boys!" he shouted. They hit a bump as they headed deep into the woods on the dirt roads that wound all through the forest.

The pickup caught air, soaring. "HOLY SHIT!" they all shouted with eyes wide and jaws open. BOOM!! All four wheels landed in the rocks and gravel, kicking up dirt everywhere. Jake never took his foot off the gas. They veered left and right until Jake got control of the vehicle. The boys laughed uncontrollably.

The police car hit the same bump. In Jake's rearview mirror, he could see a huge cloud of dust. The headlights that were following them veered off towards the right and stayed put. Jeff and Brad turned around and cheered. The cops were grounded and they weren't going anywhere.

"Whoooo!" hollered Jake. He was on a high. It felt good to lose control, to push things to the limit.

"Take that you bastards!" shouted Brad out the window, laughing hysterically. Jeff laid his head against the back window, grinning from ear to ear.

Jake reached down towards his radio and turned the guitar drenched metal music up even louder. He grabbed another beer and began to down it as they headed deeper into the woods. The buzz in his head was getting stronger and he could feel his body relaxing. It was doing the trick. His mind was numbing and he wasn't thinking about things. About all the crap.

"Well, fellas," he stated. "Shall we go find us some hunnies?" He and the guys laughed as they escaped into the refuge of the black forest.

Chapter 19

Chloe hurried home after school and rushed to the mailbox. Bills, bills, junk mail, more bills…there it was. The envelope's return address showed "Harvard University". She tore it open. Her eyes scanned the letter. And then they welled up in tears. Dear God. They had accepted her. They had actually accepted her. She reread the letter, making sure she had read it right. Chloe's heart thudded hard against her chest and she felt lightheaded. Could this be the happiest day of her life? She rushed into the house, eager to share the news with her dad.

Chloe found him on the sofa, slugging back straight Jack Daniels. His graying hair was disheveled and his thin, drawn up face was embedded with deep wrinkles. Even from where she was standing, Chloe could smell the liquor on his breath. Her dad had already been drinking for a while. He looked up at her with hollow eyes.

"Daddy, I have something to tell you." She sat down at the edge of the coffee table and tried her best to smile at him.

Bill Mayer said nothing to his daughter. He just stared back at her.

Chloe held up the letter. "I just got a letter from Harvard. They accepted me, Daddy!"

Still no response.

Chloe looked down at the letter and then back up at him. "I'm going to college next fall, Daddy. A free ride. I got one of the top scholarships. We don't have to come up with the money."

Bill Mayer took another slug of whiskey. His bloodshot eyes blinked lifelessly back at her.

Chloe could feel her happiness quickly fading into oblivion. She looked at him with disbelief. He didn't have to drink himself to death. He was already dead. "Daddy. I have the chance now to get out of this place and make something of myself. And then I can come back and take care of you."

Bill Mayer grunted. "I don't need you to take care of me." He took another drink.

Chloe stared at the shell of a man that used to be her dad. In his place was a bitter, hateful, sorrowful person. Chloe extended her hand, attempting to reach out to him.

Bill snapped his arm away and stood up forcefully, hugging his bottle against his chest. "Don't touch me!" He staggered away towards the stairs, his shoes scuffing against the carpet. And then he turned and faced her, a look of pure disgust reflecting from his sunken eyes. "You know, if you're anything like you're mother....you'll *never* make it."

His words hit her as hard as his fist did. Only, they left a bruise on her heart, not on her body. She watched him disappear up the stairs. She heard him slam his bedroom door, certain that soon he would be passed out on his bed. Chloe gulped hard and stared down at the letter. The words began to blur as tears formed in her eyes. Her hand began to tremble. She sat there for a while, her head spinning. And then cursing herself, she got up and went to her room. Chloe tucked the letter safely into her dresser drawer. Then she changed into her uniform and headed back downstairs to go to work.

Chapter 20

They had been talking for a while now. As they sat in his car, they spoke of school and friends they knew and other stuff that young people talked about. Chloe was smiling, looking down at her hands that sat in her lap.

"You look cute in your uniform," he teased.

She jokingly rolled her eyes. "Yeah, right. You think I should put my tip apron back on?"

Ty Snyder laughed. He could see now why all the guys talked about Chloe. She was different, mesmerizing. And sitting in his car, parked outside of Chloe's work, he wanted to dive in deeper, to get to the core of who Chloe Mayer really was. "So…maybe we could go to your house sometime. I could meet your dad…"

He could see Chloe instantly stiffen up. "We can't," she muttered.

Ty frowned. "Why not? What's the problem?" He knew her dad was an alcoholic and that she had a rough upbringing. Everyone knew that. But how was he ever going to have any kind of meaningful relationship with her if she didn't confide in him about things?

She fidgeted. "We just can't, ok."

Ty looked at her. Her eyes took on a whole new demeanor. They were troubled, lost and scared. The smile that radiated from her lips was suddenly gone. "Chloe…you know you can talk to me." He reached for her hand.

She pulled it slowly away from his grasp.

It disappointed him that she was holding back. She was only allowing him to see sides of her she wanted him to see, shutting the rest of herself off to him. What was it going to take? Ty took a deep breath. "I'm sorry."

Chloe looked out her window, silent.

He reached out again and touched her hair. He hated the tension he was feeling right now. "Hey," he softly replied. "Look at me."

She turned to him. He smiled at her and grazed her cheek with his fingers. Her skin was so unbelievably soft and flawless. Ty leaned in and kissed her tenderly. She began to respond. Their kiss became more passionate, making him want her yet again. They didn't get together very often. And it drove him crazy. His hand began to move up her waist towards her breasts. She stopped him and pulled away.

"What's the matter, Chloe? Don't you want this?" he breathed heavily, trying to contain himself.

She seemed embarrassed. "Yeah, I do," she quietly responded, not looking him in the eye.

He held her hand. "So what's the matter?"

Chloe still wouldn't look at him, only down into her lap. And then she slowly glanced over at him. "I, I've never…"

Ty Snyder was taken aback when he realized what she was trying to say. "Wait a minute. You mean…you're telling me…you're still a virgin?"

She looked back down again and nodded her head yes.

He saw the innocence in her and it turned him on even more. Something stirred deep inside of him, a raw emotion. He couldn't explain it. But all of a sudden, he realized *he* wanted to be the first to touch her, to make her feel pleasure like she had never known. More than ever now, Ty wanted to break through that wall she had built up around herself.

But he knew it would take time. He couldn't rush this. And so, he simply smiled at her. "I'm glad you told me. It means a lot." He kissed her hand, realizing she had just shared one secret with him. "Hey, are you hungry?" he asked, attempting to lighten the mood. "I could sure use a burger."

Chloe seemed relieved that they had changed the subject. "I could too."

Ty started up his car. They drove to a local burger joint and hung out for quite awhile, enjoying each other's company. By the time Ty dropped Chloe off at her car in Neveah's parking lot, the restaurant had long since closed and all was dark.

Chloe got out and walked to his side of the vehicle.

"So when can I see you again?" he asked. "You're a hard person to catch sometimes." He winked at her.

She leaned down. "I promise I'll be in touch." She never gave him a definitive answer. Is that why he was becoming so hooked on her? She kissed him though the window. And then Ty watched her get into her car and drive away. He smiled to himself and headed home.

Chapter 21

"You wanted to see me, Mr. Whitman?"

Peter Whitman looked up from his desk and saw Jake Stevens standing in his doorway. "Yes, Jake. Come in." He pointed to a chair.

Jake took a seat.

The plump, high school counselor looked sternly over his wire rim glasses at him. Jake simply stared back, his face expressionless. And then Peter cracked a smile. "You got in!"

Jake's face brightened. "Are you serious?!"

"Yep, a four year academic scholarship to Caltech! See for yourself!" He slid the letter over so Jake could read it. He watched as Jake scanned it, smiling from ear to ear.

"I just can't believe it! I can't believe it!" Jake was dumbfounded.

Peter sat back in his chair and put his hands behind his head. This exact moment was why he loved his job, why he loved being that stepping stone towards a brighter future. "You're a smart kid, Jake. You keep this up and you'll breeze right through medical school."

Jake stood up and shook Peter's hand. "Thank you so much, Mr. Whitman. For everything you've done."

Peter's heart swelled. He had a soft spot for troubled kids who somehow overcame life's bumpy road. And Jake was one of the special ones. He had followed Jake's progress all through high school, amazed at how somebody like Jake could really shine if he wanted to. He smiled as Jake started to leave. And then he called out. "Hey, what do you think of Chloe's deal?"

Jake turned around. "What are you talking about?"

Peter frowned. "Didn't you hear?"

It was Jake's turn to frown. "Hear what?"

Peter cleared his throat. He could see the confusion in Jake's eyes. He knew Jake and Chloe were the best of friends. But apparently she didn't share this news with Jake. And he wasn't sure why. "Chloe got a free ride to Harvard. She found out a couple of weeks ago. She didn't tell you?"

Jake looked down at his acceptance letter and then back up at Peter. His face was expressionless again. "No, she didn't."

Peter Whitman simply nodded and watched as Jake turned towards the door and left.

Chapter 22

Molly Watters was beautiful. She was blessed with silky blonde hair, fair blue eyes, and a body to die for. She always got what she wanted. And she *never* got dumped. In fact, it was normal for her to have tons of guys vying for her attention. But she didn't want a ton of guys. She wanted Jake Stevens. And she couldn't figure out why he wasn't head over heels for her like every other guy she had ever dated.

She had been nice, witty, sexual, everything a guy could want in a girlfriend. But no matter how hard she tried, she couldn't keep him. Even worse, she couldn't get him back. And worse yet, she couldn't let him go. It had been almost a month since he had lost interest. It had not been a mean or malicious break up. Jake just slowly began closing himself off to her. She could feel him slipping away from her, like sand falling through her fingers. And no matter how hard she tried, there was no holding onto him.

It was after school and she was waiting by his pickup now in the school parking lot, feeling like a stalker. But she just had to see him. She just had to talk to him again. Oh, how it hurt that he did his best to avoid at her in the hallways. Instead of looking deep into her eyes like before, he now barely glanced her way, smiling forced, weak smiles simply for the sake of being polite. She just couldn't stand it.

Before long, Molly spotted him exiting the high school. He was so handsome, tall and strong. Everything she wanted and more. When Jake got closer, he spotted her and sort of stopped. And then he walked up to her.

"What are you doing, Molly?" he asked softly, melting her as he looked at her with those deep, intense brown eyes of his.

"I thought maybe we could talk," she replied, trying her best not to look desperate.

Jake shook his head and looked down. "There's nothing to talk about."

She reached for his hand. "Please, Jake. I just want to work things out. I don't understand what I did."

He stepped back to avoid her touch. "You didn't do anything, Molly." He shook his head again. "You just…don't understand." He looked genuinely sorry.

"Well, then explain it to me! Help me to understand!" OK, she was begging now and looking extremely desperate. Passing students were glancing over as they made their way to their cars. But she didn't care. Let them stare. She wanted Jake back so badly. She wanted to feel his arms around her again, whispering in her ear, making love to her.

Jake opened his pickup door. "I can't do this now, Molly. I have to get to work." He got in and started the truck up.

In one final attempt, she shouted to him, "I love you, Jake!"

Jake looked at her with eyes that seemed to be looking through her, not at her. God, why couldn't he look at her and see who she was and tell her he loved her too? He said nothing at all as he pulled away and left her crying in the school parking lot.

Chapter 23

Upbeat music played softly on Samantha Brown's stereo. She was lying on her stomach in the middle of her bed with her nose in an open calculus book, twirling her curly, long hair around her finger. She frowned as she stared at the numbers and symbols imprinted on the pages in front of her.

Chloe sat at Samantha's desk with the same book. "Ok, let's go over these functions again," replied Chloe.

Samantha sighed, looking completely bored by the whole idea. "I say, let's take a break."

Chloe gave her a stern look. "Samantha, we've only been at this for 30 minutes."

Samantha sat up and began flipping through a Cosmo magazine. "But you're smarter than me at this stuff. You just get it."

Chloe gave her a funny look. "Well....isn't that why I'm over here on a Friday night helping *you* instead of out partying with half the high school?"

"Speaking of partying, are Brad, Jeff and Jake at 'The Hills' tonight?" Her eyes sparkled and she casually blew a big bubble with her chewing gum. It made a loud popping sound and Samantha quickly sucked it back up into her mouth.

Chloe could see she wasn't getting anywhere with her friend. She closed her book. "I suppose. I don't know."

Samantha swung her legs over the side of her bed, her voice full of excitement. "How is it that you can be *just* friends with the three hottest guys at Mason High?"

Chloe burst out laughing. "Three hottest guys?! I don't know about that!"

Samantha giggled. "Oh, come on, you have to be absolutely blind not to think that."

Chloe shook her head. "I don't know. I grew up with Jake. And Brad and Jeff? I've known them since 6th grade. It's just different. They're my good friends. I can relate to them better than most girls…except for you of course." She smiled at Samantha, thinking how nice it was to have another girl to talk to sometimes.

Samantha got up and went to her closet, sorting through all of her clothes that hung neatly on hangers. She had plenty of the latest fashions. "I guess I'm just like every other girl at school."

Chloe raised an eyebrow. "What do you mean?"

Samantha sighed. "Brad, Jeff and Jake are wild boys. We're all hopelessly attracted to the idea of being the one girl who can tame them and make them fall…"

Chloe said nothing at all. She had no idea her male friends had such an effect on the female population.

Chloe watched Samantha toss her auburn hair back and smile. She was so pretty and carefree. She had the perfect life with perfect parents, a perfect home; hell, even a perfect room with plush carpet and a pink bedspread. Chloe thought for a second what it would be like to step into Samantha's shoes.

"So…how are things going with you and Ty? He's sooo cute too," Samantha crooned, snapping Chloe back to reality.

Chloe blushed and looked down. "It's good. We don't get to see much of each other with my job and everything. But it's nice."

Samantha eyed her. "Have you guys…you know…?"

It took Chloe a second to figure out what she was getting at. And then her eyes widened. "What? Oh! No, not yet."

"What are you waiting for?" Samantha asked teasingly.

Chloe shook her head and looked down into her lap. "I don't know. I guess the right moment."

Samantha giggled. "Well you know what would really turn him on?" She pulled out a tight pair of jeans and a sexy top. "If you wore this." She handed the clothes to Chloe.

Chloe looked at the designer jeans and the form fitting shirt. "Are you crazy? I can't wear this stuff!"

"And why not? You would look so good!" Samantha pulled Chloe's hair tie loose and tousled her long locks. "You know! Let your hair down, style it a little, put a little eye shadow on and some lipstick. He'd have to have sex with you right then and there!"

Chloe's eyes grew huge. "Samantha!" She flung a pillow at her.

Samantha threw her head back and laughed hysterically. "Come on, Chloe! Haven't you ever dreamed about becoming someone different?" She grew serious, draping Chloe's hair gently around her face and over her shoulders. She stared deep into Chloe's eyes and spoke softly. "To not be yourself, to let loose, to let go? You know…forget it all." Her eyes sparkled.

Chloe stared back at her. Oh, if Samantha only knew how many times she had dreamed about that. How many times she had laid in bed, crying, praying that she could go to sleep and wake up to become a different person living in a different world.

Chloe looked at Samantha who now had a crazy smile on her face. And then she looked down at the clothes in her hands. "You really think I'd look good in these?"

"Absolutely!"

Chloe eyed Samantha who still had that crazy smile on her face. A small grin spread across Chloe's lips. "Oh, what the hell right?"

Samantha squealed with delight, jumping up and down and clapping her hands like a little girl. "This is going to be so much fun playing dress up!" She began running all about the room gathering makeup, curling irons and nail polish.

Chloe laughed gently at the chaotic scene unfolding in front of her and then she looked in the mirror that sat on Samantha's dresser. *Playing dress up.* Here she was, about to turn 18, and this was the first time in her life she had ever played dress up.

Chapter 24

It had been a couple of weeks since Chloe had seen Jake or the guys. Other than the few minutes at school between classes or during the lunch hour, they really hadn't spent much time with each other. She guessed everyone was as busy as she was with after school jobs, homework and everything else that went along with being a senior. It was easy to get caught up in it all.

Chloe's days consisted of rushing to work everyday after school, running her butt off waiting tables in order to make as many tips as she could each night and then coming home late to the usual empty house where tons homework awaited her and mounds of housework begrudgingly stared her in the face.

Her dad still worked the graveyard shift at the mines. Surprisingly, he had kept his job through the years despite his worsening alcoholism. It was a good thing that they didn't see much of each other. Their times together were never good.

By the time Chloe had finished her homework and cleaned up the kitchen, it was 12:30 when she finally managed to crawl into bed. Even though she was exhausted, she laid there for a long time, unable to fall asleep. Sleep was becoming something elusive. She was far too young to have that kind of problem. As she lay awake, Chloe imagined that other kids at her school were sound asleep and

THE DIAMOND HILLS

had been for several hours. But then again, they didn't have to worry about paying the bills, taking care of a sick, abusive parent or battling demons that appeared in the form of nightmares, all while trying to go to school and graduate. No one understood what it was like. No one...except for Jake.

Chloe looked out her window towards Jake's house. His pickup was gone. He was probably out with a girl.

Finally giving up on getting any rest, she decided to get dressed and drive up to their "secret hiding place" at "The Diamond Hills". She chuckled to herself as she pulled on a pair of jeans and a sweatshirt. After all these years, they still called it that. She loved it up there. It didn't matter whether she was by herself or with Jake, it was another world. A place where she could go to stare up at the night sky and just forget. Their "secret hiding place" had become her refuge, her escape.

Her dark blue '69 convertible mustang hummed up the winding road that led deeper into the woods. It was the same winding road that she and Jake had ridden their bikes on countless times before they both learned how to drive. She relished the cool breeze that whipped her hair and she always got lost in the road ahead of her. Smiling, she turned off her headlights and drove the rest of the way slowly in the dark, letting the lights from the stars guide her. She always did that. It made her feel like she was truly entering another world.

Through the trees up ahead, she could see that Jake was there. She turned her car off and decided to walk the rest of the way in. Chloe stopped amongst the foliage and watched him. Too consumed by his thoughts, he didn't know she was there. He was partially sprawled across his tailgate, nursing a beer and looking up at the sky. Soft music came from his pickup. He had a melancholy look on his handsome face. Yes, Chloe smiled to herself. Jake *was* handsome. He definitely wasn't that skinny, knobby-kneed little boy she had first met on their neighborhood street. He had grown up tall, muscular and strong with piercing brown eyes and dark hair. Jake was tough and rugged, a "wild boy" as Samantha had put it. And that's what all the girls were drawn to; that obscure, rebellious side. But deep down, he was still the most sensitive person she knew, always willing to put her first, no matter how bad he had it. She treasured that. She treasured *him*.

Chloe rustled some branches as she made her way towards him. He smiled when he saw that it was her. "Couldn't sleep either, huh?" he asked.

She stood in front of him, her hands shoved in her front jean pockets. "No," she replied softly. "Where are Jeff and Brad tonight?"

"Probably still at that wild party at Frank's house. Those two never give it a rest." He looked at her. "They miss you, you know."

Chloe looked down at her old biker boots. "I know."

Jake cleared his throat. "Busy with school and work…and Ty, I suppose? How are things going?"

Chloe looked back up and saw a shadow pass over Jake's eyes. "Ok."

Jake fidgeted. "From what I hear, he really likes you."

Chloe could feel herself blush and she hoped Jake couldn't tell in the dark. She just smiled and looked away.

"Just be careful, Chloe." His voice was soft.

Chloe looked back at him. She could see how much it pained him to talk about it. Each time…each new guy…it got harder and harder. For the both of them.

Jake must have sensed the awkwardness too. He shook his head and looked away. "Oh, listen to me! Who am I to warn you about potential assholes? I'm the biggest ass out there."

Chloe chuckled. "Let me guess, you ran into Molly tonight."

Jake ran his fingers through his hair and sighed. "Molly…and practically every other girl I've ever been involved with since junior high. What luck is it to have all of them show up at one party?"

Chloe laughed out loud. "You've dated a lot of girls, Jake. The probabilities are stacked against you."

Jake shook his head, a look of disdain across his face. "I guess! And every single one of them reminded me of what an ass I am."

Chloe shoved Jake's leg aside so that she could sit down next to him. "So quit being an ass," she replied matter-of-factly. She grabbed his beer and took a long swallow.

He chuckled. "And risk ruining my reputation I've worked so hard to achieve?"

Chloe laughed and playfully butted her shoulder against his. "Oh, that's right. I forgot."

They laughed tenderly for a few seconds. Jake eyed her. "You're the only girl who doesn't think I'm an ass."

Chloe drank some more beer and handed the bottle back to Jake. "Not true. I've just learned to deal with it through the years."

Jake smiled at her, his eyes sparkling. "What am I going to do with you, Chloe?"

Chloe smiled back. "I don't even know what I'm going to do with myself." She jumped off the pickup bed and slowly began walking, looking up at the billions of stars. She listened to the trees rustling in the breeze; the sound resembling a distant stream rushing across the night sky.

"When were you going to tell me?" came Jake's voice.

Chloe stopped short and turned around. "About what?"

Jake hopped off the bed as well. "About getting into Harvard."

Chloe looked down, ashamed. "I don't know."

Jake walked up to her, a serious look on his face. "We talked about this."

Chloe looked up at him. "I know we did. I guess I'm having a hard time accepting the fact that it's going to happen."

Jake looked troubled again. "You wanted it this way. You said one day, we'd have to find our own way. It was something we needed to do."

Chloe looked down again at her old shoes. "I know what I said." She looked at the trees and listened to the crickets chirping all around them. "But I'm realizing now how much I'm going to miss this place…this world you and I created to escape our messed up lives." Chloe shook her head. "God, how many nights have we spent up here, crying on each other's shoulders, comforting each other so that neither of us would go insane? No one knows what we've been through." She hung her head again. "No one ever will." She felt herself weakening. Chloe took a deep breath and looked into Jake's deep brown eyes. "Getting that letter made me realize…how much I'm going to miss you. I guess I wasn't ready to face that just yet."

Jake's face softened. He pulled her close and held her. She felt herself weakening even more. It felt so good to be in his arms. She shut her eyes, soaking it all in. He pulled back far enough to put his forehead against hers. She smelled the sweetness of the alcohol on his breath, stirring something deep inside of her.

"I'm scared too, Chloe," he whispered. "The next several months are going to fly. And so much is going to happen." He paused. "But whatever happens…I know we're going to make it." He gently kissed her on the forehead and pulled her close again. They stood there, once more lost in each other but too terrified to make another move.

Chloe could have stayed right where she was forever. Because Jake was making it all go away. The hurt and the fear, the sadness and the uncertainty…they were disappearing. His arms were her salvation. And she wanted to tell him that. She wanted to tell him everything. But instead, she pulled away. "I'm going to go now."

Jake said nothing to her. She felt his eyes burning through her as he watched her walk away.

Chapter 25

Clarissa Stevens climbed into the passenger side of the fancy, black suburban. That familiar new car smell instantly hit her nose. Her eyes quickly scanned the interior. No trash, nothing out of place, not even a layer of dust on the dash. She looked at everything in the vehicle. But she didn't look at him. She never liked to look at them. That's just how she did things. "So what do you want?" she quickly asked, spitting her gum into a piece of paper and then shoving it into her pocket.

The man began to drive. "Explain it to me."

Explain it to me? Oh, now she *had* to take a look at this guy. He wore a dark blue three piece suit, immaculately pressed with not a thread out of place. His light brown hair was graying slightly at the temples. Clarissa guessed he was 45 to 50 years old perhaps. He was definitely handsome. She also noticed he donned a shiny, gold wedding band on his left hand. She grunted under her breath. He was another rich businessman, traveling and wanting a quick lay while away from the wife and kids. *Bastard.* She rolled her eyes. "If you want oral sex, it's $20. The price goes up from there. Just don't kiss me on the mouth or mess up my hair." She pulled out a cigarette and lit it, not bothering to ask if it was ok if she smoked. She could feel him watching her as she slowly blew out the smoke. He didn't say anything, just drove. After a bit, Clarissa eyed him. "So what will it be?" she asked impatiently.

The man turned to her. His eyes crinkled as he grinned. "How about we just drive and talk?"

What the hell? She didn't have time for this! She needed her next fix and talking wasn't going to get it for her. Clarissa grew angry. "No, I don't do talking. Pull over!" She pointed to the side of the road.

He held up his hands. "Relax! I'll pay you. I'll pay you whatever you want. You'll get your money."

Clarissa glared at him. "You better not be shittin' me! I'll kill you!"

He stared at her for a second. "I'm not messing around. I promise! You just looked like you could use a ride." He looked back towards the road. "And I just wanted someone to talk to."

She slowly calmed down, dragging hard on her cigarette and staring straight ahead. He suddenly handed her a wad of cash. She stared at it and then quickly snatched it up, stuffing it into her pocket.

"I'm Randy."

Clarissa said nothing.

"Ok, you don't have to tell me your name. I can handle that." They hummed along in the luxurious vehicle with the leather seats.

Clarissa stared out at the passing scenery, wondering how long she was going to have to ride with this jerk.

He spoke up again. "I'm from Boston. On my way back there now. Just passing through your town here." He paused. "Are you from here?"

Clarissa still said nothing. She just dragged on her cigarette, trying to figure out why in the hell this guy was so interested in just talking. No one ever just wanted to talk.

He continued. "Anyway, I'm anxious to get back home. My wife's birthday is coming up. And…I want to surprise her."

Clarissa rolled her eyes again. "That's real nice, Randy. I'm happy for you." Her voice dripped with sarcasm. She continued to stare out her window.

Randy ignored her hostile comment. "I've got two little girls. 8 and 6. They're great!" Randy looked over at her. "You got any kids?"

Clarissa ignored him. They drove in silence for a few minutes more.

Randy ran his fingers through his graying hair. "I'm thinking a big bouquet of flowers, some champagne, maybe a nice dinner at a fancy restaurant. You think she'll go for that?"

Clarissa wished he would get the hint that she didn't want to talk to him, that she could care less about what he had to say. "I don't know your wife, Randy!" she snapped. She glared at him.

Randy grimaced. His eyes suddenly turned sad. "Yeah, well…the problem is…I don't really know my wife either…not anymore."

Clarissa frowned, surprised by the sudden unsteadiness in his voice.

He looked at her. "And it's all my fault."

Clarissa noticed he was gripping the steering wheel a little tighter.

"I've been so busy advancing my career, I kind of forgot about my family," his voice was shaking now.

Clarissa could see the genuine pain in the man's face. She stopped smoking her cigarette and continued to listen.

His eyes alternated between the road and Clarissa as he spoke. "I mean, here I am, the CEO of a million dollar company where everyone practically bows in my presence." He drew in a breath. "And my wife…my wife says she's going to leave me! She going to take my little girls and leave me because I've never been around for them!" Randy was visibly upset now. "And she's right! She's absolutely right! My God! What am I going to do? What's this going to do to my wife? Not to have her husband?" He turned to Clarissa, tears quickly filling up his eyes. "What am I going to do without my precious little girls? They're so young, so impressionable! How's this going to affect them? The world is so messed up anyway. And now they're not going to have their daddy!" Randy sort of lost it then, weeping as he drove.

His words reverberated in Clarissa's head. She knew all too well what would happen to his family. They'd fall apart. Just like hers did. Clarissa looked down at her dirty, scabbed up arms and her filthy clothes. Jesus, how did she get here? What had happened to her? She used to be happy a long time ago. She had a life, people who cared about her, a reason to wake up every morning. Now her days consisted of finding her next high or her next drink and whatever it took to get it. Out of nowhere, Clarissa started to cry too. And then like a crazy woman, she blurted out. "I have a son! He's graduating from high school this year!"

Randy quieted his sobs long enough to look over at her. Clarissa looked over at him with bloodshot eyes. "Other than that, I don't know much about him." She covered her mouth with her hands. "My God! I'm his mother and I don't even know anything about my son!" She wept into her hands then, leaving Randy staring at her, dumbfounded, not sure of what to do or say. Clarissa couldn't stop crying. Randy finally pulled the vehicle to the side of the road. Clarissa choked on her tears. And then she looked back at Randy, wiping her eyes with the back of her hand. "It's too late for me, Randy. But it's not too late for you. You've got to make things right. For your wife…for your little girls." She fumbled for the door.

He reached out for her. "Wait! Where are you going? Are you going to be alright?"

Clarissa said nothing as she sobbed hysterically, yanked the door open and disappeared onto the streets.

Chapter 26

The ringing phone on Jake's night stand startled him out of a deep sleep. It wasn't every night that he was able to sleep so soundly and so he cursed as he reached for it in the dark. "Hello?" he mumbled, his eyes still closed.

"Jake. It's Officer Jenkins."

Jake sat straight up in bed, suddenly wide awake, a sick feeling creeping into his stomach.

"I'm sorry, son. You're going to have come down here again."

Jake hung up the phone and sat in the dark, his face in his hands. Oh God! Not again! This just wasn't happening! He quickly got dressed, hopped into his pickup and headed towards downtown. He pulled up to the county jail and walked in. He said nothing as Officer Harry Jenkins strode up to him.

"We picked her up at the Quick-Stop on 5th and Horton. She was pretty strung out, throwing things around, screaming at the top of her lungs."

Jake just looked at Officer Jenkins. It wasn't anything he hadn't heard before.

Officer Jenkins shook his head, a look of disgust in his eyes. "You shouldn't have to do this, son. It's not right…"

"Just show me where she's at!" hollered Jake. He was angry. He hated this part. He absolutely dreaded it and he wanted to get it over with.

His abruptness shut Harry Jenkins up. He grabbed his keys and led Jake through several doors before they got to the holding cells. This particular facility housed only women. As they made their way down the long corridor, the women in the cells starting whooping and hollering at Jake.

"Hey, sweetheart. Come here, baby!"

"Little boy, let me turn you into a man!"

"You wanna get laid, sugar? I got what you need right here."

They bombarded Jake with vulgarity. Jake tried his best to ignore the whistling and all the cat calls from the whores and drug addicts. He wanted to sink into the floor. But he followed Officer Jenkins to the last cell at the end. Because in there was another whore and drug addict—his mother.

She was sitting on a bench, her head in her hands. The other women who shared the cell all looked at Jake with interest. It wasn't every day that a good looking guy like him showed up.

"Clarissa...you're son's here," called out Officer Jenkins.

Clarissa slowly looked up at Jake. Her eyes were bloodshot with dark circles under them. She looked like death warmed over. She slowly walked up as Harry Jenkins unlocked the door. Clarissa barely glanced up at Jake as she brushed by him. Jake shook his head and walked with his mother, enduring the obscene harassment from the other women until they were in the clear.

Officer Jenkins grabbed Clarissa's arm to get her attention. "I don't want you back here, Clarissa. You're not going to get out as easily next time, you understand me?"

Clarissa jerked her arm free and glared at him. "Can I have my damned cigarettes now?" She extended her hand.

Harry shook his head incredulously, reached behind the counter and slapped the pack into her palm. He gave Jake another sympathetic look, one of many that Jake was growing to hate. Jake just turned and walked out with his mother. They got into the pickup and drove off.

Clarissa lit up and stared out the passenger window.

Jake looked over at her. Her hair was greasy and stringy. Her clothes were soiled with dirt and unmentionable stains. She reeked of sweat, sex and drugs. "Jesus, Mom! You look like hell."

She ignored him.

"You know, I have a stinkin' test tomorrow morning, Mom. I should be home sleeping, getting my rest. But instead, I'm out in the middle of the night picking up *your* ass from the pound!"

"Go to hell," she muttered.

"No Mom! You go to hell! YOU GO TO HELL!" Jake was losing it now. He was so angry, he was shaking. "How many times are you going to pull this shit?! Huh?! Until they call me up to go and identify your body down at the morgue?!"

Clarissa rubbed her head. "Jesus, here we go again."

Jake stared at his mother in disbelief. She had nothing. No emotion, no heart, no love. He shook his head. "I can't believe this. I can't believe you. What happened to you, Mom? How did you become such a cold person?" His emotions got the best of him. He started to cry. Damn it! He told himself he wasn't going to lose control. But he couldn't stop. It just hurt. It hurt so badly.

Clarissa fidgeted, staring at him. She yelled, "What the hell do you want from me, Jake!"

Dear God. He was going to tell her. Jake shouted, "For you to love me, Mom! I'm still that little boy waiting for you to love me!" He choked. "Why couldn't you ever just love me?!"

Clarissa rocked back and forth in her seat, covering her ears with her hands. "Shut up! Shut up! I can't handle this right now!" Her voice was quivering. Her body was shaking. "Pull over! Pull over!!!" She was screaming at him now, grabbing for the steering wheel.

"Stop it, Mom! Stop it! You're going to kill us!" He struggled with her, trying to hold her off. The pickup veered all over the road. Horrible screeching noises emanated from the tires.

"Pull the truck over! Pull it over!!!" She was hysterical now, pounding her fists on him, on anything she could swing at.

Jake had no choice. He skidded to a halt on the side of the road. Before he knew what was happening, his mother had bolted out and was running down some back alley. Jake got out. "Mom! Mom! Come back! I'm sorry! I'm so sorry!" Jake screamed after her, crying his eyes out. Jesus Christ! What was he supposed to do? He was just a kid! He had always been just a kid! What the hell was he supposed to do?

Jake felt a tremendous anger building up inside of him. He screamed at the top of his lungs and slammed his fist into the side window of his pickup, shattering the glass into a million pieces. Shards of glass pierced his knuckles and palm, making him scream even louder. He stared through blurred vision at the red blood that pooled in his hand. Jake looked around, not really seeing anything at all, even though there were street lights and buildings and a few passing motorists. His head was in a thick fog and he knew he had to get out of there fast. His shoes crunched on broken glass as he got into his pickup and skidded back onto the road.

Chapter 27

She was dreaming. But for once, they were not nightmares. They were vivid dreams that only came when a person was in a deep, deep sleep. Then the rustling and the creaking noises sounded in her ears, invading her mind and incorporating themselves within the images she was seeing. Someone was at her window, crawling in. Chloe bolted upright in bed, trying to focus in the dark on the shadow standing in her bedroom. "Jake? Jake, what's the matter?" He was shaking, visibly upset, watching her.

She got out of bed and walked over to him. He was holding his right hand, wincing from the pain. Even in the darkness, she could see that his eyes were red and swollen and fresh tears were running down his cheeks. The rag he had wrapped around his palm was soaked in blood. "Oh my God! What happened?" Trying to remain calm, she tenderly looked at his palm and sat him down on the edge of her bed. She quickly ran to the bathroom and came back with some peroxide, cotton balls and gauze. With the utmost care, she unwrapped the bloody rag and looked at the gash. "Jake, you've got to get stitches! You're bleeding…"

"No!" he shouted. "I'm not going anywhere!" His hand shook uncontrollably. His voice shook as well.

She knew he wasn't thinking straight. She could see the madness in his eyes. And so she didn't push it. "Ok, ok. Let me see what I can do." She swabbed the wound with the antiseptic. Jake moaned in agony, his good hand holding the wrist of his hurt hand. "I know! I'm sorry!" she apologized. She felt horrible for his pain. But she did the best she could, cleaning the blood and then carefully wrapping his hand tightly with the gauze. In the darkness of her room, she could see that Jake was pale. He looked lifeless. She touched his cheek with her fingertips. "What happened, Jake?"

The madness in his eyes glinted at her. "She ran off, Chloe! And I didn't go after her! I just let her go!" Jake began to shake again. "What the hell kind of person does that? I'm such a horrible son!" He cried, his shoulders heaving.

Chloe shook her head and put her hands on his face to calm him down. "Don't say that, Jake! You're not a horrible son! Please stop crying!" She sat down next to him and wrapped her arm around his shoulder, trying her best to sooth him.

Jake sobbed, explaining his night to her. This was the 4th time in 3 months he had had to endure this humility. He rubbed his eyes and his voice was strained. "I'm so tired, Chloe. I'm 18 years old and I'm so damn tired." He leaned his head on her shoulder and whimpered like a little kid.

She wrapped her arms around him and squeezed him tightly. "I know, Jake. I know you are." Her heart truly ached. And seeing him lose it like this was especially difficult, because he was usually the rock, the brave one, her protector.

Chloe rocked him gently, closing her eyes and wishing she could take all his pain away. "Come on. Come lay down with me." She crawled into her bed and pulled him towards her. Jake laid his body beside hers, his head on her shoulder, his arm wrapped around her as if he was holding a teddy bear. She embraced him tightly against her, rubbing his hair with one hand, kissing him gently on the forehead as he slowly began to calm down. "It's going to be ok, Jake. Close your eyes and go to sleep now. I'm right here…" She continued to whisper comforting words to him until she felt the tension in his body leave and his breathing turn deep and steady. Finally he fell asleep. Chloe wiped the single tear that rolled down her cheek. Looking up at her ceiling, she realized there was nothing, absolutely nothing she wouldn't do for him. He was her everything. She kissed him one last time, held him tighter and fell asleep.

Chapter 28

Bill Mayer slowly shuffled into the house. He threw his empty lunchbox on the counter in the kitchen and headed up the stairs. His clothes were filthy with coal mine dust and his body ached with every step he took. Damn he was tired. Every shift seemed longer, more labor intensive. He couldn't wait to get a drink. Drinking made all his problems disappear.

Through the living room windows, he could see that daylight was breaking. The sun would be up in another thirty minutes or so. *Christ.* How long had it been since he stepped foot outside during the day? His job on the nightshift for the past ten years had turned him into a night owl. He hated the sun. People who had normal lives went out into the sun. People who had purpose went out into the sun. People who had families and were happy went out into the sun. Bill cursed under his breath. He didn't have any of that. He rubbed his face with his dirty hands. Screw 'em all anyway.

Bill walked by Chloe's room. Her door was halfway ajar. He peeked in and froze. Jake and Chloe lay wrapped up in each other's arms, fast asleep on her bed. He was holding her, lying halfway on her body. She had him in a full embrace. Even though they were both fully clothed, seeing his daughter like that made Bill's blood boil. Was this what she did when he was out working all night?

Turning into a whore? Anger came so easy for him. He clenched his fists, wanting to pummel the two of them.

Bill never liked the fact that Chloe was friends with Jake, Brad and Jeff. Maybe it was okay when they were in sixth grade but now....? Despite hiding it underneath baggy clothes over the last several years, Chloe had turned into a beautiful young woman. Any fool could see that, even Bill, as much as he hated to admit it. Her features were absolutely stunning, something she obviously inherited from her mother. And Jake, Brad and Jeff? Well, Bill remembered what it was like to be an 18 year old male. Nothing but rampant hormones and sex on the brain 24/7, wanting to screw anything that moved. Did Chloe really expect him to believe that her friends didn't look at her in that way? Bullshit! For all he knew, she was probably screwing all three of them every night. He stared at Jake and Chloe soundly sleeping. Supposedly they were the best of friends. *Best of friends*?? Hmmf! He should beat the shit out of Jake right now, just wake him up and kick his ass.

But he decided to wait. As enraged as he was, he knew this wasn't the right time. Bill stared at Chloe, vowing that she would pay for this. If he had anything to do with it, he would make sure that his daughter didn't turn into one of *those*. By the grace of God, he would beat it out of her. She would come to see the error of her ways. Bill took a deep breath, unclenched his fists and headed towards his bedroom.

Chapter 29

Jake felt someone gently shaking his shoulder. He looked up and saw his strung out mother staring down at him, crying and asking him "why?" over and over. Jake's heart began to pound. She was running away again, running far away! He tried to stand up to run after her. But he couldn't move. He couldn't move a thing no matter how hard he struggled.

And then someone was shaking his shoulder again. Jake jerked awake, startled, staring around at the unfamiliar surroundings through blurred vision.

"Jake! It's ok! It's just me!"

Jake looked towards the voice and saw Chloe standing over him, a concerned look on her face. His eyes slowly began to focus.

"We have to get to school," she replied gently.

Jake laid back down and realized he had fallen asleep on Chloe's bed. He rubbed his face with his hands and felt the pain shoot up his right arm. He jerked his hand back and saw the gauze. Everything was coming back now. His mind was remembering. God, he was tired. His body felt like it had been hit by a freight train. He looked over at Chloe. She was already dressed and ready to go.

She smiled at him. "Come on. I'll fix you something to eat." She extended her hand. He took it and let her pull him to his feet. "How

THE DIAMOND HILLS

do you feel?" she asked.

"Like shit," he responded dully. He followed her quietly down the stairs, careful not to wake her dad.

Chloe headed towards the kitchen and placed a pan on top of the stove.

Jake felt antsy and dirty as well. He wasn't very hungry. "Listen, I'm going to go home and take a shower. I'll see you at school ok."

She seemed disappointed but nodded understandingly at him. And just as he was about to walk away, she came up and hugged him tightly. He wasn't expecting it but it felt good. He hugged her back, breathing in her sweet smelling hair.

"Are you going to be ok, Jake? I was so worried about you last night." Her voice was full of concern.

He pulled back and looked at her. "Yeah, I'll be ok." He was remembering everything now that she had done for him. How she had cleaned his wound with the utmost care, how she spoke words of comfort into his ear, how she had held him so tightly. He was going to be ok. And it was all because of her. He kissed her gently on the forehead and grinned. "I'll see you," he softly replied. He left her standing there, knowing she was watching him walk up the street towards his empty house.

Chapter 30

Ty was on top of her, kissing her all over, feeling her softness against him. She was driving him crazy, especially since they didn't get together very often. She tasted so good; her kisses were deep and passionate. He wanted her more each time. He pushed himself against her, knowing she could feel the full extent of his arousal. She moaned softly, trembling. He reached underneath her shirt, feeling her firm, flat stomach and her small waist. Kissing her neck, he slowly moved up. She wasn't stopping him. He felt her bra. My God, it was lace. She was so damn sexy underneath it all. His fingers grazed the tops of her breasts and felt their fullness. Ty's mind began to race. What did she look like under there? His touch felt perfection. And to think....she had never been there with anyone else. He wanted to be the one. Was she going to let him in? With his other hand, he reached for her pants to unbutton them. Her hand quickly stopped him.

"No..." she whispered.

His heart sank. "Come on, Chloe. I want you so bad," he whispered in her ear.

"Not yet. Please stop." She was pushing him off, sitting up.

Ty hung his head down, trying to catch his breath, concentrating on making the ache stop. He finally sat up, leaning his head back against the car seat. He was a little perturbed. How many times had she done this now? He looked at her and frowned. "What is the problem, Chloe? Do you not like me or something?"

"Yeah, I like you." She was readjusting herself, straightening her top.

Ty stared at her. "Are you thinking we need to get know each other better? Because I've been trying." He felt huffy. "You're not exactly the most open person about yourself you know. You won't tell me anything about your past or what you're thinking or what bothers you or makes you happy. It makes it kind of hard to get to know the real you." Maybe he had said too much. But he had to let her know.

Chloe didn't say anything. She just looked at him, still surrounding herself with that invisible wall she had built around herself apparently a long time ago. "Can we just go now?" she quietly responded.

Ty let out a sigh, shaking his head. He started up the car and headed towards "The Hills". Out of the corner of his eyes, he stole a glance at Chloe. She wore no makeup, pulled her hair back in a ponytail, and wore baggy, unrevealing clothes. She was tough as nails and could probably kick any guy's ass if she wanted to. But she was also sensitive, kind, smart, quiet, sensual and undeniably gorgeous in the most captivating way. That's what kept him wanting more and more. Chloe was not like any other girl he had ever dated or slept with or whatever. She was so different. And he couldn't crack her code. The more time he spent with her, the more he wanted to get inside her head, inside her pants, inside her world. He wanted to be the one…

She was looking out the passenger window, avoiding him. He didn't want her to be mad. Ty reached for her hand. "Let's have fun tonight ok? I'm sorry. No more pressure. No more me going off on you like that."

She turned to him and looked as if she was assessing the situation. He was relieved when she finally smiled at him and took his hand. "Ok," she told him softly.

Another infamous party at "The Diamond Hills" was in full swing by the time Ty and Chloe pulled up. They walked hand in hand towards the swarms of kids who covered every inch of the secluded clearing. Ty began drinking, loosening up, and laughing. Chloe remained quiet, looking around at all of the people, just like she always did. If someone came up and talked to her, she was polite. But she didn't get loud and rowdy, no matter what Ty did. Even after a few drinks in her, she still kept to herself. Ty wondered if she was ever going to let her hair down.

Just then, Ty heard a ruckus nearby as some girls excitedly pointed out that "they were here."

"Who?" asked Ty.

"Only the three hottest guys in school," one of the girls immaturely crooned. Her girlfriends hollered in agreement.

Ty and Chloe looked towards the distance. Coming down the hill, Ty could see the outline of Jake, Brad and Jeff as the three of them walked like Greek gods towards the crowds of people, generating a lot of attention from all of the females they passed. Practically every girl made a futile attempt to catch their eye. It was almost as if they were rock stars or something, making their way through hordes of groupies.

Ty watched as the three guys began scanning the area, looking for fresh meat perhaps. And then they spotted Chloe. Jeff threw up his arms and in a drunken slur shouted, "Chloe Mayer! Get your ass over here!" Jake and Brad laughed at their friend but waited to see what Chloe would do. Ty waited too. He saw her blush and then a huge smile began spreading across her lips. She looked at Ty innocently. "I'm going to go say hi. I'll be back," she quietly told him. She let go of his hand and began walking over to the three guys.

From a distance, Ty saw the smiles grow wider on all of the guys' faces as if they had just found one of their long lost buddies, their missing link. Jeff ran up to her, grabbed her around the waist and swung her around like a crazy person while Jake and Brad laughed. Chloe laughed too, more so than Ty had seen her do all night. She suddenly seemed to come alive. Jeff put her down and the four of them stood and talked, forgetting about everyone and everything around them.

Ty stared in disbelief at Chloe. She was completely opening up, laughing, cutting up with her friends, being loud and rambunctious. Her imaginary, protective wall had disappeared. That wall Ty could not tear down for anything. And her three guy friends simply walked up and with no effort at all, were bringing out the Chloe Ty had unsuccessfully been working so hard to find.

What was it with the four of them? They were so tight, like nothing he had ever seen. Did they dig her like he did? Were they curious about her too? Did they want her like he wanted her? How could they not? Ty looked around and saw that everyone else at the party was staring at the four of them too. He knew they were probably wondering about the same things he was.

Ty found himself growing jealous as he watched the four of them interact. He wanted what they had with Chloe. It wasn't fair! He waited for Chloe to return to him. Instead, Ty watched as Chloe playfully jumped on Jeff's back for a piggy back ride. She let him carry her off in the opposite direction as Jake and Brad followed, leaving all the disappointed girls staring after them in dismay and jealousy.

Chapter 31

Chloe felt at home. She was with the only people in this whole world she trusted. The only people who accepted her for her, screwed up or not. And most of the time, it was screwed up. But that was ok. They didn't care. They never cared.

Jeff ran with her deeper into the woods, carrying her on his back. She kept her legs and arms wrapped tightly around him, like a little kid. The music and voices from the party were fading into the night behind them. She could hear Jake and Brad following them, talking and laughing about something. They had all been drinking. She could tell Jeff was pretty drunk. He was slurring, telling her about his crazy night and the girl that had blown him off for no apparent reason at another party they had just come from.

"Why did you leave? You should have stayed and fought for her," Chloe commented.

Jeff slowed down, letting Jake and Brad catch up. They were passing around a bottle of Jack Daniels. Chloe grabbed the bottle and slugged some back, still hanging on to Jeff.

"We had to come find you. It's no fun without you," Jeff slurred.

Jake laughed. "You drunk asshole! Tell her the truth! She blew you off because you were breathing Jack into her face and grabbing her boobs!"

THE DIAMOND HILLS

Brad howled with laughter. "Damn, they were big, weren't they? She was hot!"

Chloe grinned. "You screwed up, Jeff." She adjusted her grip around his neck.

Jeff slyly smiled. "I know. I always do that." They found a beaten path that wound deeper into the trees and the four of them followed it.

Chloe looked up at the night sky. The stars sparkled back at her. She closed her eyes, smiling.

Jeff's crazy voice interrupted her quiet thoughts. "Did you see all their faces back there, Chloe? You know damn well what they were thinking, don't you?!" slurred Jeff. Even though he was drunk, he was still strong, carrying Chloe with ease as they all walked.

Chloe opened her eyes, unsure of what Jeff was trying to tell her. "What are you talking about? You're not making any sense."

Jake and Brad laughed, shaking their heads. Apparently, they seemed to know what Jeff was getting at.

Jeff lifted Chloe higher onto his back and started laughing too. "Everyone back there thinks we're all doin' you! I mean here we show up, kidnap you from the party and disappear into the woods. Chloe Mayer's gotta be our love slave. Why else would they keep her around? That's what they're thinkin'!" Jeff shouted. He laughed even harder.

"You're wasted, dude," stated Jake. He slugged some more whiskey back.

It didn't even phase Chloe. She knew her friends like the back of her hand. And it made her angry that everyone was trying to judge her anyway, let alone her relationship with her friends. Why couldn't they just leave well enough alone? They had no clue about her. They had no clue about any of them. "Let them think what they want. I don't care." Her tone was short and bitter.

Jake and Brad glanced over at her, a surprised look on their faces.

Jeff put her down. He must have sensed something deeper was bothering her as well. "Ok, what's the matter?" he asked. The four of them stopped and sat down in a grassy patch, passing the bottle around.

"Is it Ty?" asked Brad.

Jake stiffened. "Has he tried anything?"

Chloe looked embarrassed. But she knew she could trust her friends. "He's trying. Maybe a little too hard." And she didn't mean just the physical end of things. Chloe reflected back on what Ty had told her earlier in the evening, about her not letting him in.

Jake looked the other way.

Brad frowned. "Give us the word, Chloe. And we'll take care of it."

Chloe shook her head. "I can handle it." She looked in the direction from where they had just come from, back towards the party. "I just get so tired of people who think they've got it all figured out. And it's not just Ty. But everyone. The way they look at me, at all of us." She shrugged her shoulders. "So let them keep wondering why you guys keep me around. It's just something else for them to try and figure out." She grinned at her friends.

Jake and Brad looked at her and smiled.

And then Chloe chuckled. "Besides, I'm supposedly screwing the three hottest guys in school according to the female population at Mason High." She rolled her eyes sarcastically.

Brad playfully punched Jake in the arm. "Did you hear that?!" He laughed.

Jake simply grinned and looked down.

Jeff laid his head on Chloe's lap and looked up at her, making himself at home. "I love you, Chloe," he slurred.

It was Jake's turn to roll his eyes. "Oh, shit. Here we go again."

Brad snickered. "You're such a sap when you drink, Jeff! If you're not grabbing some chick's boobs, you're confessing your undying love to Chloe."

Chloe laughed as she looked down at Jeff, his face softening as he stared back at her. She knew he was completely harmless. This had happened countless times before. "You *are* drunk, aren't you?"

He gave her a goofy grin. "It's true. We all love you. But especially me. I really love you, Chloe."

Jake grunted. "I need to take a piss." He got up and walked off.

"Make that two of us," replied Brad. He disappeared too.

Jeff continued his drunken banter. "I mean, you're the only girl who hasn't broken by heart."

Chloe rubbed his hair. "Oh, that's sweet, Jeff. But aren't you usually the one who breaks all the girls' hearts?" She could hear Jake and Brad laughing at her comment as they peed amongst the trees.

"That's not the point, Chloe. I'm telling you that I love you. And I hope that you're still saving yourself for me. Don't give it to that jerk, Ty. He doesn't deserve you. You're too special to give it to him."

Chloe laughed and drank another shot. The guys knew she still hadn't slept with anyone. "Can we quit talking about this?"

Jake and Brad came back then, having heard the whole conversation. "Come on, buddy. Let's walk this off a bit," Jake replied. He helped Jeff to his feet and they began walking down the path.

Grinning from ear to ear, Brad shook his head and sat down next to Chloe. "Jeff's crazy."

Chloe looked after them. "Yeah he is. But I love him too." She truly meant it. She cared deeply for her friends.

Brad grew serious once he knew it was safe to talk. "Hey, is Jake going to be alright? He wouldn't tell us much about what happened with his mom."

Chloe had noticed too that Jake still had his hand wrapped. "I think he'll be ok. He's just worn out."

Brad looked down at the bottle of Jack. "I know Jeff and I don't share the same relationship with him as you do. But I wish he'd open up to us more sometimes."

Chloe intertwined her arm around Brad's and leaned her head on his shoulder. "Oh, he thinks the world of you two. But you know how it is amongst guys. He feels he's got to be tough and insensitive. With me…it's different."

Brad shook his head in agreement. "It is different with you. I mean, Jeff jokes that we all love you. And we do. We'd do anything for you. But Jake? Man. I think if anyone ever tried to hurt you, he would go absolutely insane." He locked eyes with Chloe. "What he feels for you, Chloe, no one can touch. Like it's sacred or something, you know?"

Chloe swallowed hard. She knew exactly what Brad was saying. She felt it too. Before they could continue talking, Jake and Jeff were stumbling back.

"I need to get laid. I need to find me a girl," slurred Jeff.

Jake was laughing. Chloe stood up and held onto Jeff's arm. "Well, despite what everyone thinks, you're not getting any from me so we better head back to the party."

Jeff looked Chloe in the eyes. "You're so straight with me. You tell it like it is. That's why I love you Chloe."

"Yes, I know, Jeff. I love you too." She looked over at Jake who was smiling at her. She smiled back at him and the four of them headed back towards the party. Chloe was sure she could hear all the girls squealing with delight when they showed back up.

"Right there. Right over there. The brunette who's staring at me." Jeff pointed over at a group of girls.

"I'll go with him," responded Brad, shaking his head at his brash friend. He helped Jeff stagger away, leaving Jake and Chloe standing amongst the crowds of people.

Chloe looked over at where she had last left Ty. He was still there with his friends, looking over at her, smiling. Wow. He wasn't mad. She looked back at Jake who was giving her that look. That look that said he didn't want her to go. "I better get back," she told him.

"Ok," his deep voice responded.

"Thanks for coming to find me."

Jake nodded.

She turned to leave. And then she felt his hand grab hers. She turned back around, her heart racing.

"Are you going to be ok?" he asked, his eyes serious as could be.

"Yeah." She squeezed his hand reassuringly and then let go. Ty watched her as she strolled back over to him. By the time she got to his side, she could see that Jake had disappeared into a sea of people.

Chapter 32

Jake's hand began to throb. Man, he had really screwed it up. But he supposed it was healing, slowly. Had it already been a week? His mother still hadn't shown up. Was she dead? He had no idea. It made him sick to think about it. So he took another slug of Jack Daniels to numb his mind.

People were all around him. Dance music pulsated through the night air. How long had he been standing here? He couldn't remember. Jake watched all the kids from his school and some that drifted in from somewhere else. They all laughed, danced and drank. Not a care in the world.

Someone was talking to him. And then another. And another. He vaguely heard their words, but responded none the less to their conversations. His eyes scanned the area. Brad and Jeff were hooking up with some girls. They would be getting laid tonight, no doubt. Other girls were trying to catch *his* eye, smiling and flirting with their tight jeans and even tighter tops. They were everywhere. He should be elated that they all wanted him. But Jake felt nothing. In fact, he was growing more numb with each sip of whiskey.

A girl appeared out of nowhere, smiling at him, standing next to him. She was telling him something about how good he looked. He smiled back at her, pretending to listen intently. His eyes found

Chloe. She was surrounded by a group of people. Ty was holding her against him. He was smiling, his face inches from hers. She was grinning back at him. And then they were kissing each other. Jake looked away.

He decided to focus on the girl who was coming on strong. She was pretty with big blue eyes and long red hair. He put his arm around her and she eagerly pressed her body against his. Before long, Jake found himself whispering in her ear about going some place quieter. She was willing, just like all the others had been. Jake took her hand and led her away. Deep down, Jake knew it wasn't right. He was using them, making them believe that they meant something to him.

They were in somebody's vehicle. He was kissing her now, making her breath harder. She was straddling him, taking off her top. He knew what to do. He had mastered it. *Look in their eyes, run your fingers through their hair, touch them in all the right places. Make them think they're the only one.* She was unbuttoning his pants, pulling him out and stroking him. Lust took over. He kissed her hard on the mouth. The girl took her panties off and slowly sat down on him. Jake closed his eyes. This was always the part where he escaped to that secret place in the back of his mind. The secret place where *she* was always at, waiting for him.

"My god, you're amazing," the girl moaned. She was riding him up and down.

Jake kept his eyes closed and his head back, fantasizing. He could feel it building up, ready to explode any minute. And the girl thought it was because of her. *They all did*. Through the fog in his head, he heard her start to scream with pleasure, throwing her head back, arching her body and thrusting her breasts out. Jake gave her everything he had. And then he felt himself let go. Pure lust. He held onto her, not because he cared. But only because she expected it. He hated himself for this. Hell, he didn't even know her name! Now, he had to come up with the excuses. He didn't want to be in her arms. He wanted to be alone.

Jake left her there. He was completely drunk now. Staggering, he made his way back to the party. Where the hell were Jeff and Brad? He was ready to go. He *had* to go, before the girl came looking for him, wanting more. His friends were gone, probably screwing those girls they picked up on. Damn it! He knew he wasn't fit to drive.

Someone else was coming up to him, wanting him. They were everywhere. Jake pushed her away, only to find someone else trying to hold his hand, trying to drag him out to dance. He didn't want to dance.

Jake made his way through the crowds. Where was Chloe? He had to talk to Chloe. She was gone too. And damn, he was drunker than shit. Jake looked down at his throbbing hand. It was hurting again. He looked at his other hand. Miraculously, it still held the bottle of Jack. He lifted it up to his lips and took another sip. His head was spinning. The loud pulsating music filled his brain and thumped like a drum. Jake sat down right where he was. Someone would take him home. They just had to. Because the whiskey wasn't working so well anymore. And he was having thoughts again. Thoughts he tried hard to suppress. Thoughts of his dead father. Thoughts of his doped up mother. Jake laid his head in his hands, trying like hell to block out the images. He had to get away. Get away from it all.

Chapter 33

Chloe kissed Ty goodnight. She watched him drive away. And then she headed into the house. She was tired and ready for bed. She walked into the dark living room. Someone flicked on the lamp. Her dad sat there with a bottle in one hand. He stared at her with bloodshot eyes. The smell of liquor was strong in the air.

"Daddy, what are you doing here? Shouldn't you be at work?" Chloe asked, startled.

Bill grunted. "How can I go to work knowing that my only daughter is out whoring around?"

Chloe froze. "What are you talking about?"

He stood up and staggered towards her. "I've been watching you. Out with that boy, doing things with him in his car." His voice shook with anger.

"You've been following me?" Chloe was astounded.

"I've seen things! Shameful things! And not just with him." Bill stepped closer. "You're screwing Jake and Brad and Jeff aren't you?" He pointed his finger into her face.

Chloe's heart began to thud. He was seriously drunk. His breath stunk of whiskey and his eyes were furious. "Daddy, they're my friends. They would never think of…"

"Shut the hell up! I'm no idiot! I can't believe the things that have been going on while I'm away all night at work!" He took another swig of alcohol.

Chloe felt her anger rise. "You don't know what you're talking about!" She frowned. "And since when have you cared about what's going on around here, let alone with me?! All you care about is that damned bottle of yours!"

Bill's eyes turned black as coals. "I am your father! You have no right to talk to me like that!"

"Daddy, you haven't given a shit about me since I was a kid! Why should you care now?" Her voice was turning into a high pitched shrill. "You have no idea what's going on! You don't know anything about me or the type of person that I am!" She was shaking now, angry that he was accusing of her something she could never be.

He got into her face. "I will not have a whore for a daughter!"

Chloe screamed at him. "I'm not a whore!"

"Shut up you whore! You're just like your mother! You stinkin' whore!" He punched Chloe in the face with his huge knuckles and threw her against the wall.

Chloe felt the pain radiating from her cheek all the way down to her mouth. Something in her mind snapped. She jumped up and began pummeling Bill with her fists. She pounded him in the face, head, body…anything she could hit. He wasn't expecting it. He fell to the floor, trying to shield the blows. Chloe jumped on top of him, punching him and kicking him with all of her might. She screamed obscenities at him at the top of her lungs. Chloe had lost it. She was out of control. She was through with him hurting her. She had had enough. Damn it! She was not a whore! She was not all the things he thought she was! He had no idea who she was!

The blood spewed out. It didn't matter that he was moaning in pain. She couldn't stop. The skin on her knuckles busted open and bled. She felt nothing. And so she kept pounding, kept kicking…with all that she had in her.

Finally, something in her made her quit. Chloe fell to her knees, completely spent, her heart racing so fast she thought it might burst.

She was crying, screaming at him, not knowing what was coming out of her mouth. In a blur, she saw him pull himself up off the floor and stagger out. Blood was on the rug, on the couch, in the doorway. She vaguely heard him drive away.

Chloe cried in the middle of the living room floor, her knuckles burning. Her right eye and lip throbbed. She wanted to throw up. Her head was spinning. She saw her dead mother in the bathtub, blood dripping from her slit wrists. "Why did you leave me in this hell!" Chloe screamed out loud. No one was listening. No one was around. She was alone.

It seemed like an eternity. Or had it just been a few minutes? Chloe dragged herself up. She saw the blood. She cried all the way to her car. She cried as she backed out of her drive and sped down the road.

Chapter 34

Samantha Brown ran as fast as she could towards the party. She prayed they were still here. It was so late and this was the only place she figured they would be. Frantically, she looked around at the crowds of kids who were mostly drunk. The normal craziness had died down. Music still played. But everyone was mellow, coming down from their evening high.

Her heart pounded against her chest. "Where the hell are they?" she asked more to herself than to anyone. Finally, she spotted them. Jake, Jeff and Brad were sitting on the ground, surrounded by a bunch of girls, their usual harem of admirers. She ran up to them. "Jake!"

Jake looked up at her. "Samantha?" He must have picked up on the worried, frantic look on her face. He immediately stood up. "What's the matter?" Brad and Jeff stood up too. Suddenly, all of them seemed very sober.

"It's Chloe. Something's wrong!" She was breathless, trying to hold back the tears that wanted to flow. Samantha was so scared.

Brad frowned. "What are you talking about?"

Samantha tried to control the shaking in her voice but the tears were spilling out from her eyes now and down her cheeks. "I stopped by her house tonight. There's blood! Blood everywhere! And her car's gone!"

Before she could finish talking, the three guys had bolted out of there, making a b-line for Jake's pickup. Samantha didn't know what to do. She was utterly terrified. Something bad had happened. Something really bad.

Chapter 35

They had searched everywhere, everywhere they could think of, even Jake and Chloe's secret hiding place. She was no where to be found. They also saw the blood, the busted lamp, the turned over chairs. "It was Bill," stated Jake, feeling that sickness in his stomach again as they scanned the living room. Only they didn't know whose blood it was.

"Think, Jake! Where else could she be?" hollered Jeff. They all drove off in the pickup, tearing down the streets, hoping the cops weren't out. It wouldn't have mattered anyway. They had to find their friend.

"What if she's in the hospital?" asked Brad.

"Don't say that! She's ok! Just shut up and let me think!" Jake was so upset, he was shaking. And then, shockingly, he thought of a place in the woods. It had been awhile since they all were out there. He remembered how the forest stopped and a huge cliff overlooked a deep valley. Chloe had morbidly joked how if anyone ever wanted to jump, it would be the perfect place to do it. Call it a sixth sense. Call it a hunch. Jake couldn't explain it. He just knew. He gulped hard. "I think I know where she's at." He turned the pickup around and headed up the mountain.

Daylight was starting to break as they tore through the forest as fast as the winding road would let them, not saying anything to each other. Finally they started to reach the edge of the woods. In the distance they spotted her car.

Jake skidded to a stop. The three guys jumped out of the pickup and ran towards the clearing. Chloe was there, standing at the edge of the cliff, so close to going over that they all held their breaths. She was staring down at the valley below, the trade winds whipping her hair and jacket around wildly. The night sky in front of her was slowly turning orange, emitting an eerie glow all around her body.

They all approached her cautiously and slowly, afraid to startle her. "Chloe…what are you doing?" Jake called out, trying to keep his voice calm.

And as if in slow motion, she turned and looked at her friends. They saw the huge cut on her cheek and the busted lip. Her eyes were red from crying. She looked as if she was in a trance. She slowly turned back forward and stared back down over the cliff, inching a little closer towards the edge. Rocks and pebbles were falling over to the deep valley below.

The guys stood rigid, steadying themselves, each one of them ready to dive for her if they had to. "Come on, Chloe. Come over here and let's talk about what happened," called out Brad.

"I could have killed him. I could have killed that son of a bitch," Chloe's voice was surprisingly calm and steady. She turned to her friends again. "I *should* have killed him." Her eyes flashed a hint of madness.

Jeff took a deep breath. He was scared shitless. They all were. "You're going to be okay, Chloe. Come with us." He held his hand out, trying his best to reach out to her.

Chloe ignored them. They watched as she closed her eyes and arched her head up. She held her arms out like a bird expanding its wings. Her body teetered dangerously on the edge, especially when the wind gusted. "It would be so easy…so easy to just fly away. Fly over the edge and make it all go away…" Her voice was soft and low.

Jeff and Brad flashed Jake a terrified look. Jake couldn't stop shaking. "Jake!" whispered Jeff vehemently.

Jake held up his hand to them, blocking out everything else around him and focusing only on Chloe. Every nerve in his body was wound as tight as humanly possible. Jake was prepared to save her. Even if it meant going over with her. She wasn't going to leave him like this.

"So easy, so easy…" she repeated, her eyes still closed, her arms still outstretched.

The guys were too shocked to say anything. They just stood, hoping and praying that they wouldn't have to see their friend jump. "Please, Chloe! You can't do this!" screamed Jake silently in his head. But outwardly, he knew he had to remain calm.

"So easy…" Chloe whispered one last time. She braced her body, ready to jump. The guys' eyes grew to the size of grapefruits. And then…she dropped her arms and opened her eyes. She turned to her friends. "But then again, when has anything come easy for me?"

They stared in disbelief as she walked away from the edge. She looked beaten, defeated and tired. "I'm not gonna jump," she mumbled to them, looking down at her feet. It sounded as if she was almost disappointed in herself. Without another word, she bypassed them, got in her car and tore out of there.

"Jesus Christ!" muttered Jake. He plopped down on the ground, holding his head in his hands. Waves of nausea hit him. He felt lightheaded.

Jeff began tearing up, his eyes watering profusely. He walked several feet away so the other two wouldn't see him.

Brad let out a huge breath, running his fingers nervously through his hair. "That was close, Jake. That was way too close." He looked at Jake whose body sat motionless on the grass.

Even though he heard Brad's words, Jake couldn't respond. He was trying to fight the waves of nausea in his gut. And he was still trying to come to grips with the fact that he had almost lost his best friend.

Jake looked up at the horizon. The sun was coming up now, its bright rays signaling the start of a brand new day. A brand new day full of hope and promise. Jake hung his head down sorrowfully. Was there such a thing as hope and promise? Especially for people like him and Chloe? Jesus Christ, he had almost lost her. Her mind was so far gone she was ready to jump, ready to leave it all behind. Jake shuddered. Maybe it was too late. Maybe he had already lost her.

Chapter 36

It was Monday morning. And Chloe was walking through the halls of her high school. The kids were staring at her, whispering in front of her, behind her, all around her. It had spread like wildfire. The whole school knew.

"Did you hear?" they were saying. "Chloe Mayer got beat up and almost killed her old man Saturday night. What a freak!" Nothing new. They just glanced at the cuts and bruises and looked the other way. *Stay away from the girl whose crazy mother killed herself and whose alcoholic father wants her dead.* At least, they'd leave her the hell alone.

In the middle of 4th period, Chloe was called to the principal's office. When she got there, she saw Mr. Whitman, the counselor, and a police officer all standing next to Mr. Jackson's desk. Chloe could only guess what this was all about. They all stared at her like she was a sideshow freak.

"Sit down, Chloe," replied Mr. Jackson, as he pointed to a chair. He couldn't tear his eyes away from her wounds.

Chloe didn't say a word as she slumped down. She didn't want to be here. She didn't want them staring at her like they were doing.

Mr. Jackson placed his hand on the police officer's shoulder. "This is Officer Thompson."

Chloe looked at the young man standing in front of her. He looked like a rookie with his baby face and his light brown mustache. His face softened, like he felt sorry for her or something. "Hello, Chloe. I thought I should talk to you in person."

Chloe glared at him, waiting for him to continue.

"You're 18 now. And what you did to your father, you would be tried as an adult for assault and battery with the intent to inflict bodily harm." He sat down on the edge of Mr. Jackson's desk, leaning in close as if he was trying to get her full attention. "That can carry a serious sentence."

Chloe didn't flinch. She just continued to glare at him.

Officer Thomson cleared his throat and leaned back. "But your father has decided not to press charges."

Chloe looked away. Tears started welling up in her eyes. Damn it! Why did all of this hurt so much?

Mr. Jackson spoke up. "He's still in the hospital, Chloe. Maybe you should…"

"I don't want to see him!" she spat. Her lip quivered. The tears rolled down her cheeks.

Peter Whitman sighed heavily. "Chloe, I know this isn't your fault. Nobody's blaming you." He pushed his wire rim glasses further up his nose. "Your father is an abusive alcoholic. Nobody should have to go through what you've been going through."

Chloe wiped her tears with the back of her hand, not wanting to look at their faces, knowing she would see looks of pity and sorrow. Damn it, they had no idea! They had absolutely no clue!

Mr. Whitman looked down at his shoes. "Maybe you should talk to someone. A professional." He took his glasses off this time and held them in his hand. "They could help you deal with all of this. *We* could help you."

Chloe looked at the three men standing in front of her. Officer Thompson and Mr. Jackson were nodding in agreement over Mr. Whitman's comment. And just as she thought, they all had looks of pity and sorrow on their faces.

Chloe stood up, took a deep breath and looked all of them square in the eyes. "No offense, Mr. Whitman, but you're all about 10 years too late." She turned and left them standing there dumbfounded.

Chloe somehow made it through the rest of the school day. She simply just shut out everyone around her, concentrating only on what she needed to. She grabbed her books from her locker and headed out towards the parking lot. Someone was calling her name. It was Ty. He ran up to her and stared at her face.

"My God, Chloe. Why didn't you call me?"

She could tell he was at a loss of what to do. He didn't know how to handle it. "It's alright. It's over with." She turned to leave.

He grabbed her arm. "It's not alright! Half your face is beat up! And I have to hear about it from people in the hallways?"

She pulled her arm from his grasp. "I don't want to talk about this now, ok. I've got to get to work."

He frowned. "When are you going to talk to me? When are you going to let me help you?"

She grew angry. "You can't help me!"

Ty ran his fingers through his blonde hair, frustration written all over his handsome face. "Look, I understand what you must be going through…"

She glared at him. "Don't! Don't *even* say you understand…because you don't!" She didn't want to hurt him like this. She could see it his eyes. He was trying, but deep down, he was lost, so out of his territory. His uneasiness was so evident. It wasn't worth dragging him into this. She sighed and squeezed his hand. "I'll talk to you later, ok? I really have to go now."

Chloe knew Ty was watching her as she made her way to the guys who were waiting for her in Jake's pickup. They had all witnessed what had just happened. Chloe got in and slammed the door. She looked over at Ty. He was standing right where she left him, an angry, confused look on his face. He shook his head and walked away. Chloe stared out the window so the guys couldn't see how upset she was even though she knew that they all knew. Nobody said anything as Jake started up the pickup and drove away.

Chapter 37

"Do you think she'll show?" asked Brad. He, Jake and Jeff were at another party at "The Hills".

Jake shrugged. "She said she would. She said it would be good for her to get out." Jake stared into one of the bonfires that was burning. "I just don't know. Maybe it's too soon."

"What about her old man?" asked Jeff. He took a drink from his beer bottle.

Jake shook his head. He could feel the anger creeping back into him. "Who knows? He's like my mom — MIA." He looked at his two buddies. "I don't think he'll be beating up on her anymore though."

Brad shook his head. "What an asshole."

Jake agreed. If it were up to him, he would have killed the bastard a long time ago. Then maybe none of this would have ever happened. Jake sighed. "I'm going to get some more beer from the pickup." He walked to his vehicle and reached inside for the six pack. Just then, he saw Chloe pull up in her blue mustang. Wow, she *did* show. He strolled up to her.

She got out and gave him a weak smile. "Hey," she replied softly.

"Hey," he replied back. In the moonlight, he could see that her lip was still a little puffy and bruised and the cut under her eye was slowly getting better. Even so, she didn't look good. He sensed her uneasiness. "How are you?"

"I'm ok. How are you?" she asked.

"I'm fine."

She looked down at his hand that was still bandaged up. "You should have gotten stitches. It's taking way too long to heal."

Jake grinned. "Would you quit worrying about me? It's you I'm worried about."

Chloe looked towards the party and all of the people.

Jake grew serious. "You know, you don't have to do this."

Chloe shook her head. "No, I want to."

He smiled at her again. "Ok."

They walked together towards the crowds. Chloe hung out with her friends for awhile. But they could tell she was still shaken up. She kept to herself even more so than usual. She didn't laugh at all and she hardly smiled. Jake could see that the looks she was getting from everyone was making her nervous and uncomfortable. People were gawking and still whispering about what had happened. Any loud laughter and playful screaming made her flinch. She couldn't relax. They were all worried about her.

"Hey, do you wanna leave? We'll take off," replied Brad. He put his hand gently on her shoulder.

Chloe shook her head. "No, I'll be alright. I see Samantha over there. I'm going to go say hi."

Jake, Jeff and Brad watched as Chloe made her way through the crowds of kids to the other side.

"She's not good," replied Jeff, keeping his eyes on her, just like Jake and Brad were.

Jake took a swig from his beer. He kept quiet as he wiped his mouth with the back of his hand.

Chapter 38

Chloe wished that she could just relax. But she was on edge tonight. Everyone that bumped into her accidentally made her tense up. She would shield her face as if she was afraid someone was going to strike her. It was ridiculous. She felt like an idiot. She had to get over this. It was just another party. She had been to so many. Life had to go on. But the music was so loud and the laughter was ringing in her ears…

Samantha smiled at her as she walked up. "Chloe! How are you?" She hopped off the tailgate she was sitting on and threw her arms around Chloe, hugging her.

Chloe stiffened. Jesus, it was just Samantha. *She's not trying to hurt you*. Chloe quickly forced herself to hug Samantha back.

Samantha pulled away and smiled at Chloe again. She climbed back up on the tailgate and patted the spot beside her. "Come on."

Chloe sat down, trying her best to relax.

Samantha looked at her bruises, her face growing serious. "I'm so sorry this happened to you."

Chloe looked down at the ground. "Jake told me how worried you were."

Samantha nodded feverishly. "I was. I was so scared. I didn't know what to think, Chloe. I didn't know what to do."

Chloe didn't say anything.

Samantha cleared her throat and dropped her voice. "What happened, Chloe?"

Chloe stiffened a second time. She hadn't told anyone except for the guys. But something in Samantha told Chloe that she could trust her. It was so nice to have her to confide in. "He was drunk, accusing me of horrible things." Chloe paused. "I guess I just lost it when he hit me."

Samantha didn't say anything. She just listened intently.

Chloe looked Samantha square in the eyes. "I got tired of being that terrified little girl."

Samantha sat there, soaking it all in. She nodded towards Jake, Jeff and Brad. "Well, I must say. You have some really good friends over there. They really care about you, Chloe. They've been watching you like a hawk."

Chloe looked over at them. Samantha was right. What would she do without them?

Samantha whispered low again. "It's killing Jake, you know."

Chloe turned to Samantha.

Samantha continued. "That he wasn't there to stop it."

Chloe looked back over at Jake whose eyes connected with hers for a split second and then looked away.

A group of girls walked by then and stared at Chloe. Samantha and Chloe overheard one of them whispering, "That's her."

Samantha rolled her eyes, giving them a dirty look as they quickly moved on. "What is wrong with people?" She was angry.

Chloe gently touched her arm. "It's alright, Samantha. I'm used to it."

Suddenly, someone being rowdy bumped into Chloe. In an instant, Chloe was flinching and shielding her face.

Samantha sensed Chloe's uneasiness. "Come on, let's go get a drink."

The two girls hopped down from the tailgate and began making their way to the keg. The ringing was beginning again in Chloe's ears. Crap! She had to get through this. She had to make it all better. She just couldn't let herself slip...

Some guy came up to her then, touching her back and trying to come onto her. He was severely intoxicated.

"Please, leave me alone. I'm not interested ok." Chloe tried to be polite. She turned to walk away.

"Come on, baby. Don't blow me off." He was trying to take her hand, stroking her back at the same time.

Samantha grew worried. In the distance, she could see the guys making their way over.

"Stop it. I just want to get a drink." Chloe did her best to distance herself from him.

"Come on. You know you want to be with me." He was grabbing her arm now, trying to pull her towards him. They were starting to cause a scene as other kids stopped to watch.

"Don't!" Chloe was trying to shove him away. But the guy was relentless.

"Just leave her alone, ok!" yelled Samantha.

"Why don't you just stay out of this!" he hollered back. He yanked Chloe towards him and tried to kiss her. "Come on baby! You know you want it! I'll give it to you!" He puckered up, raining kisses down on her face, his grip around her tightening.

Chloe squirmed. "Stop it! Stop it!" What the hell was wrong with him? Didn't he know she was trying to get through all of this? She was trying to be ok again! And he was hurting her. Just like her dad had hurt her.

Chloe's mind snapped again. "You son of a bitch! Get the hell away from me!" She wriggled out of his grip and punched him hard in the nose. So hard in fact that the guy fell backwards onto the ground. Even though she was looking right at him, Chloe couldn't really see him. He was a blur, just like everyone else around her.

Jake, Jeff and Brad ran up just in time to see blood spewing out of the guy's nose. He was holding it, moaning in agony and screaming that his nose was broken. Everyone was watching and everyone was in shock.

Chloe was furious. "You son of a bitch! Don't you ever touch me again!" she screamed. Suddenly, everything came back into focus. It was then she realized what she had done and that everyone at the party was staring at her. She was that little girl again. The freak that all the kids at school were scared to hang out with. Tears stung Chloe's eyes. Her mind was racing as incoherent images flashed crazily in her brain. She had to go. She had to get out of here.

Chloe broke through the crowds of kids and sprinted to her car. Everyone watched in disbelief as she disappeared, leaving nothing but a cloud of dust behind her.

Chapter 39

She was curled up on her side in a fetal position lying on the cool grass. Her eyes were closed. His mind flashed back to when they were kids and how they used to lay in that exact same spot, talking to each other, being there for each other because they had no one else. Twigs snapped underneath Jake's shoes as he slowly made his way to her. He carefully laid down on his side next to her, watching her face like he always did.

Chloe opened her eyes and stared at him. Fresh tears rolled down her sad face.

"Brad and Jeff wouldn't leave me alone until I made sure you were ok," his voice whispered soft and low.

"I'm so sorry, Jake."

"Shhh. You have nothing to be sorry for."

The tears spilled from her eyes. "I don't want to be that person. I don't want to go crazy like my mom. I don't want to be so angry like my dad. What if it's too late for me?"

Jake reached out and stroked her hair. "It's not too late, Chloe. You're not going to be that person. I won't let that happen. Remember? We promised each other." Chloe nodded and he knew that she did remember. They had made a pact that they would be there for each other, get each other through all the bad things, do whatever it took to keep each other sane.

Chloe sniffled and she began to tremble. "I'm so scared. My mind. It's messed up. Like there are all these pieces that are..."

"Shattered," he finished her sentence for her. She stared at him in disbelief. Yes, he experienced it too. The fragments, the gaps, the distorted images that invaded every crevice of his brain. He whispered, "It scares me too. But you know what I do when that happens?"

She looked deep into his brown eyes.

"I think of you." He pointed to the side of his head. "You're always here...waiting for me, ready to make it all go away."

Her face softened. Her eyes glistened with new tears. She reached out and stroked his cheek gently. "You're the most amazing person, Jake Stevens."

He closed his eyes and put his hand on top of hers, relishing the softness of her touch. It was just them now. Escaping into that place. That place that no one knew about. Jake listened to the sound of his beating heart and the breeze that rustled the trees. He heard the billions of crickets chirping all around them.

She whispered to him, "I wish I could become a totally different person. Somebody else who's nothing like me." She paused. "I'd look different, act different, *be* different. I'd go far, far away where no one knows me."

Jake kept his eyes closed and listened to her soft voice. He knew exactly how she felt. Life had to be better then this. Being someone else had to be easier than this. He opened his eyes and looked at her battered but beautiful face. "It's going to be ok, Chloe. We'll make it. We're going to make it." And with his bandaged right hand, he took her right hand. Her knuckles had busted open again and small droplets of blood were oozing from them. They intertwined their fingers, staring at their wounded hands. Chloe and Jake remained perfectly still as they laid side by side underneath the stars that shined down upon their secret hiding place.

Chapter 40

He had called it quits, breaking things off with her. It had been a couple of weeks now. They were officially done.

Ty had had enough. She just wouldn't budge. God, how he had wanted her! He had wanted all of her. But she stopped his hands. She stopped his questions. She stopped *him*, Ty Snyder, the guy that no girl had *ever* denied.

So enough was enough. He had to call it quits. But the funny thing was that she didn't even seem upset. Hell, she seemed almost relieved. *Relieved*?! No one who ever got dumped by Ty Stevens was ever relieved. They begged and pleaded for him to take them back. Only to be shoved aside and left crying with a broken heart. Now it was Ty who felt shoved aside. She had broken *his* heart. He never thought that was humanly possible.

Damn her! He wanted her more than ever now. He wanted her all to himself. She had done something to him, to his mind. Jealousy like he had never known before flooded his emotions. He didn't want anyone else to touch her, to kiss her, to screw her. He wanted to screw her.

Ty was drunk now, sitting alone in a chair in some mansion of a house. How did he get here? And whose house was this anyway? Ty grunted. Ah, who the hell cares? It was just another stupid party where the alcohol flowed and all the kids went wild, looking for someone to get lucky with. Ty took another slug of whiskey. It seemed the more he drank, the more he thought of her. And the more he thought of her, the more he wanted her. And the more he wanted her, the angrier he got that he didn't have her. Shit, he was seriously drunk.

Suddenly he heard a commotion. More people were walking through the door. Ty looked up. Shit. No wonder the girls were all going wild. The "three hottest guys at Mason High" were walking in. Ty snorted. Bastards. They were all pricks. He hated them. They seemed to have it all. Good looks, all the girls they wanted and of course, Chloe....Chloe. Holy shit. There she was.

She had walked in last, behind all of them. And shit, she was smiling. She was actually smiling. Was she that happy to be rid of him?

Ty stared at her. No makeup, baggy clothes, hair in a ponytail. The most beautiful girl he had ever laid eyes on. He knew every asshole here wanted to get into her pants. Wanted to see what was underneath all that. Damn, he wanted to see what was under there too. He had felt some of it. If it looked as good as it felt....Ty took another swig. He watched her, lying low.

She hung close to her friends. They were like her damn bodyguards or something. He had to find a way to talk to her. Maybe, just maybe she would take him back.

Ty waited. He let everyone mingle and get a few drinks in them. He was careful to keep himself hidden. Pretty soon, the guys were off hooking up and Chloe, well Chloe was walking off on her own, getting ready to head outside to meet up with some friends. Now was his chance.

Ty peered out into the mammoth back yard. Lights were strewn along the bushes and trees, illuminating the kids who where mingling and enjoying each other's company. He scanned the crowds of people, looking for her. She was talking to Samantha and a group of girls. Ty felt his heart pounding. He slugged some more whiskey back and headed outside.

Chloe had her back to him when he walked up to her. Her friends all kind of glared at him. They all knew he was the one that had dumped her.

Chloe turned around, almost shocked to see him standing there. "Ty, how are you?" she nervously asked.

Ty looked at her, ignoring the hateful glares her girlfriends were giving him. "Can I talk to you for a second?"

Chloe looked to her friends and then back at him. "Ok," she softly responded.

She followed him. He led her away from the crowds towards the very edge of the yard. It was dark, secluded and quiet. They found a bench and sat down.

Ty stared at her. "I've been thinking about you a lot lately."

Chloe looked away and began to fidget. "Ty…"

"I miss you, Chloe. I miss you so much." He knew he sounded desperate, but he just didn't care.

Chloe shook her head. "I thought you said it was over."

Ty took her hand. "I know what I said. But I was an idiot. Please, Chloe…"

Chloe pulled her hand away. "It's just no good, Ty. It's not going to work out."

He felt his heart sinking. "Don't say that! Please, Chloe. I want you back. I want you so bad…" He reached out to kiss her.

She pulled back. "Stop it, Ty. You're drunk. You don't know what you're talking about."

He pulled her towards him. "I do know what I'm talking about. I want you, Chloe. Please, just let me touch you…" He began kissing her face until he found her mouth. She was driving him crazy. He had to have her. He shoved his tongue in her mouth, pushing his body against hers.

She began fighting him. "Ty! Please. Stop it! Stop it!"

But Ty couldn't stop. The more she pushed him away, the crazier he got. No one else was going to have her. Only him. He would be the one. He pushed her down on the bench and pressed his body on top of hers, feeling her curves underneath him.

"Get off of me! Please!" She was squirming with all of her might.

But he had her pinned just right. She wasn't breaking free. And he was strong. He had never been more aroused, more turned on. It didn't matter that she had a look of horror on her face. Once he got inside of her, she would enjoy it. She would realize what she had been missing. And she would beg for more. Ty shoved his tongue in her mouth and reached under her shirt. He grabbed at her full breasts, kneading them with his hands. She tried to scream but it came out muffled as he kissed her harder. He began tugging at her pants, feeling them slipping down past her waist and hips. His hand felt cotton panties. He was almost there. She was kicking and squirming underneath him. "I know you want it, Chloe," he managed to say as he mauled her with his mouth. He reached down to pull himself out. God, he couldn't wait. He had to have her right now….

Someone was grabbing him and before Ty knew what had happened, he was flying through the air. His right wrist made a gruesome popping noise as he landed on the ground. Ty rolled flat onto his back, the wind completely knocked out of his lungs. He looked up and saw Jake standing over him. POW!!! A blow so hard smashed Ty in the face that he heard the bones in his jaw shatter. Ty looked up at Jake in horror again. Jesus Christ! Another one was about to come…

Chapter 41

Jake jumped on top of Ty and began pounding him with everything he had. He could feel Ty's bones breaking underneath his knuckles but he didn't care. A piece of Jake's mind was shattering, just like he and Chloe had talked about. The fury in him was so fierce that he just couldn't stop. Couldn't find that safe place where Chloe was at. Chloe wasn't there this time. Instead, she was crying on the bench, half naked, violated and almost raped of her sweet innocence. "You bastard! You almost raped her! What are you trying to do…strip her of the one thing she's got left in this godforsaken world?!" Jake screamed at the top of his lungs at him. He couldn't see. He wasn't aware of the crowds of kids surrounding them, staring in horror as Jake continued to pound on Ty like a mad man. He wanted to kill him. He wanted to put him six feet under. He would have done it too. He would have beaten Ty Snyder to death that night had it not been for Jeff and Brad who somehow managed to pull him off.

"You son of a bitch! You almost raped her! You almost raped her!" He was lunging towards Ty's broken and beaten body that lay lifeless on the neatly mowed grass. Jeff and Brad were doing their best to hold him back.

Chloe covered her mouth and cried as Samantha came to comfort her. They watched as Jeff and Brad had to drag Jake away while some of the other kids ran to Ty's side. He was unrecognizable. His face was a pool of blood. "Someone call 911!" one of them yelled.

Jake broke free from Jeff and Brad's grip. He ran up to Chloe, grabbing her by the shoulders. "Chloe! Did he hurt you?! What did he do to you?!"

Chloe shook her head, her eyes wide with fear. "We gotta go, Jake! The cops are going to be looking for you."

Jake looked like a crazy person. His eyes were wild. He looked confused, angry, distraught.

"She's right, Jake! We gotta split!" hollered Jeff.

Jake grabbed Chloe's hand. They all ran out of the house and to their vehicles. Everyone apparently realized they had better leave too. Cars and trucks squealed and peeled out in every direction. It was pure chaos as everyone made a fast getaway.

Five minutes later, Jake, Chloe, Jeff, Brad and Samantha were in Jake's living room.

"What are we going to do?" asked Samantha. She was so scared, sitting next to Chloe on Jake's couch, wringing her hands together. "What are we going to tell the cops?"

Jake was pacing the floor. He turned and glared at Samantha. "He almost raped her! What would they expect me to do?"

"That doesn't matter, Jake! You almost killed him! Hell for all we know, he could already be dead," hollered Brad. He ran his fingers nervously through his hair.

"Oh, my God. I can't believe this is happening..." cried Samantha. She put her face into her hands.

"Just calm down!" replied Jeff. He stood up, rubbing his forehead. "Maybe no one will say anything."

Brad looked at him incredulously. "Are you nuts?! There were 200 kids at that party. They all saw what happened!"

Jeff held up his hands. "I'm just saying they all knew what Ty was trying to do to Chloe..."

"I can't believe this is happening," repeated Samantha. She wrapped her arms around herself and began rocking back and forth.

They all began arguing, yelling at each other, trying to hash out what had just happened and what they thought was going to happen. All of them except for Chloe. She sat on the couch, crying and covering her ears with her hands. Finally, she had had enough. She ran off into Jake's room. Her abrupt exit made everyone suddenly stop arguing and yelling at each other. Jake looked at all of them, feeling horrible. He went after her.

She was sitting on the edge of his bed in the dark, whimpering. Jake kneeled down in front of her. "I'm so sorry, Chloe. Please, stop crying." He realized tears were forming in his eyes as well. His voice cracked. "I just had to make him stop. God, Chloe. He was hurting you. He was trying to…" Jake cried. He was losing it now. He put his head in her lap. She leaned down and rested her head on top of his.

"What if they take you away from me?" she whispered.

"I promised you a long time ago that I would protect you, no matter what. I had to protect you, Chloe. He was hurting you. I couldn't let him hurt you anymore." Jake sobbed like a little kid. He didn't know what else to do.

Chloe couldn't stop shaking as she wrapped her arms around him. They both cried in the dark, terrified of what was going to happen next.

Chapter 42

As predicted, the cops launched a full blown investigation, interviewing as many students as they could. But miraculously, no one was talking. Nobody saw anything, nobody knew what had happened. All they knew was that they found Ty Snyder lying in his own pool of blood, beaten up by somebody…but no one had seen who it was. The kids at Mason High realized what had almost happened that night and what would happen if anyone talked. So they all kept silent.

Ty Snyder spent a week in the hospital and then out of the blue, he mysteriously transferred to another school in another state. Just like that, he was gone. He must have known better than to speak the truth.

Jake and the rest of the group laid low for quite a while, not showing up at any parties, not causing any trouble. The trail slowly turned cold. The cops quit asking questions and finally the case was dropped. Everyone realized they had all dodged a silver bullet.

"It's gonna get better. It's got to get better now," Chloe reassured him. "From now on, no more fights, no more cops, no more tears. I just want to smile again. I just want to be happy."

Jake wholeheartedly agreed. Both he and Chloe had been through enough drama the last several months to last a lifetime. He was tired of it. It was time to let it all go. He couldn't change his mother. Chloe couldn't change her father. They just had to deal with it the best that they could. Soon enough…it would all be over.

And so slowly they all tried their best to get back to normal by staying busy with school and work, hanging out with each other, with other friends, and having fun again. Before long, they had all fallen back into their everyday routines.

Chloe's dad was gone. She had no idea where he was or what he was doing. The house and everything that went along with it was all on her now. At 18 years old, she was responsible for making the house payment each month and paying all the bills. But that was ok. Things seemed better without him around. She could come and go without stepping on eggshells. No more flinching or shielding her face, not knowing if he was going to blow up at any minute.

Unfortunately, Jake wasn't so lucky. His mother still showed up at home from time to time, raising hell, puking on the lawn, passing out in the house. But Jake would just calmly deal with her until she was gone again, leaving him wondering about the next time she would be back.

One of the things that helped Jake and Chloe deal with their burdensome problems at home was hanging out with their friends. They cherished the times they all had with each other, because they didn't have to worry about anything. They could just let loose and have fun.

And so here they all were on another Saturday night, cruising down the streets of their hometown. Only tonight was going to be a little different. Chloe had invited Samantha, Tracy, Jenny and Brooke to tag along with her and the guys. Tracy had been begging for an opportunity to hook up with Jake. So Chloe thought, "What the hell?" It was about time these girls found out how she and the guys did things.

Twenty minutes later, they all found themselves deep in the woods, walking on a worn path that was almost hidden by the underbrush. The night air was cool on their skin. Chloe felt so alive.

She loved it out here. She led the group, climbing hills and scaling rocks like a mountain lion.

Samantha huffed and puffed, trying her best to keep up. "Chloe! Slow down. You're killing me here." Samantha looked behind her. Tracy and the other two girls looked like they couldn't understand how being out here could be any fun. But having the company of Jake, Jeff and Brad seemed to make them tolerate it nonetheless. Tracy looked completely enthralled with Jake. Samantha smiled and shook her head.

"Come on, Samantha! We're almost there!" Chloe called from over her shoulder. She took off up the hill in an athletic sprint, her lean, strong body disappearing. Samantha stopped and put her hands on her hips, breathing heavily. Jake and Tracy caught up to her.

"She's amazing," Samantha said to them. Jake simply grinned.

They all made their way up to a breathtaking clearing. It seemed they were on top of the world. Samantha looked around for Chloe. Where was she? "Chloe! Chloe!" she hollered, hearing her voice echoing all along the mountains and valleys that surrounded them.

"Over here!" came Chloe's voice. Samantha followed the sound of her voice. She spotted Chloe standing on a huge, fallen tree that stretched across a deep ravine below.

"Oh my God, Chloe! What are you doing? You're going to fall!" hollered Samantha back towards her.

"Come here! You've got to see this!" Chloe called to her.

"Are you crazy! I'm not getting up there!"

Chloe put her hands on her hips. "Samantha, come on! You won't regret this."

Samantha looked around at the others. The girls just shook their heads thinking Chloe was absolutely insane. But the guys…the guys just smiled. To them, she was just being Chloe. Samantha took a deep breath. "All right!" She awkwardly made her way towards the huge trunk. Even with her best attempt, she struggled to climb up. "How did you get up there?!"

Chloe reached down and helped her up with ease. "Now stand up."

Samantha slowly stood, wobbling as if she was drunk. Her heart pounded like a tin drum. "Wow, this is really something," she nervously replied.

Chloe grinned. "Wait till you get out here."

Samantha's eyes grew huge. "No, I can't go out there! I'm terrified of heights."

Chloe held her hand out. She had a serene, calm look on her face. "I won't let you fall."

Samantha was scared to death.

"Trust me, Sam. It'll be worth it." She never took her eyes off of Samantha.

So Samantha took Chloe's hand and watched with horror and amazement as Chloe started to walk backwards on the old tree trunk. Samantha let Chloe lead her slowly as she calmly talked to her, reassuring her that everything was going to be o.k. Before Samantha knew it, they had made it all the way out to the middle. Samantha felt the cool breeze whipping all around her. She was shaking but she had never felt so alive.

Chloe must have felt the exhilaration too. "Cool, huh?" she responded calmly, grinning from ear to ear.

Samantha nodded fiercely, terrified to move.

"Now, look down…," Chloe whispered.

Samantha's eyes grew huge again. She followed Chloe's gaze down to her feet and then past the tree trunk that they were standing on. And Samantha saw dense fog. Eerie fog so thick beneath their feet that it was impossible to see what was down below or just how far up they were. "Holy…" she breathed. She had never seen anything like it before. It made her feel like they were floating. The two girls stood and stared down for awhile, admiring the mysterious beauty of it all.

Chloe sat down on the fallen tree and helped Samantha safely sit down too.

Samantha looked around and below them off a little ways where the guys and their dates were. They were all sitting down on the grass, talking to each other. The moon was so bright, they could see everything around them. "I can tell you've spent a lot of time out here."

Chloe looked up at the stars. "Since I was a kid. Jake and I know these woods like the back of our hands. Up here, all your problems seem to disappear. I absolutely love it."

Samantha smiled. And then she looked down at the girls. "I'm not too sure if Tracy, Jenny and Brooke love it so much."

Chloe looked down and saw Tracy sweeping a bug off her pant leg with disgust. Chloe and Samantha laughed. "Well at least she's got Jake to keep her company. She doesn't seem to mind that at all."

Samantha sighed. "Yes, but he's about as interested in her as he is in me."

Chloe grinned. "How can you tell?"

Samantha flashed Chloe a smile. "Because…he keeps looking up here at you."

Chloe frowned, a confused look on her face.

Samantha shook her head in amazement. She leaned in close so that the others couldn't hear. "Haven't you ever wondered why Jake Stevens, the hottest guy at school, has *never* had a steady girlfriend or been in a serious relationship?"

Chloe said nothing.

Samantha whispered, "Because he wants you!" Her eyes glistened.

Chloe rolled her eyes. "You're crazy."

Samantha giggled. "I've seen him, Chloe. The way he watches you, the way he looks at you. The way he just lights up whenever you come around. He doesn't act that way around anyone else."

Chloe shook her head. "You don't know what you're talking about. We've been best friends since we were 7."

Samantha shrugged. "I may not know a whole lot about calculus but I am smart enough to know that Jake Stevens…" She leaned in closer to Chloe. "…is crazy in love with *you!*" She looked over at Jake who was glancing up at Chloe. "See what I mean?" Samantha whispered.

Chloe blushed. Samantha started to giggle which made Chloe giggle. Pretty soon they were laughing out loud.

"What are you two talking about up there?" hollered Jake. He was grinning from ear to ear.

"Just girl stuff!" Samantha hollered back. She was loving this.

Chloe looked down, obviously embarrassed, and just shook her head.

"Well, are you two gonna stay up there all night or are you going to come join our party?!" yelled Jeff. He had his arm draped around Brooke.

Chloe smiled. "Come on, Sam. I'll help you get down."

Chapter 43

It was getting late and everyone figured they had better start heading back. Jake wrapped his arm around Tracy as they walked. She snuggled closer to him. She was pretty and nice to talk to. But other than that, he really didn't have any intentions of going further with her. He looked over at Brad and Jeff. They seemed to have a different idea about the girls they were with. He recognized the lustful looks they both had in their eyes.

Chloe and Samantha seemed oblivious to everyone around them. Walking ahead of everyone, they were laughing and having fun. It was so good to see Chloe smile again. She seemed to really enjoy Samantha's company.

Suddenly Chloe turned around and faced everyone. "I'll meet up with you guys later," she announced abruptly. And in a flash, she took off running through the woods, off the beaten path that they were all walking on.

Brad yelled after her. "Come on, Chloe! You always do this and then we end up waiting on your ass while you go scouting in the middle of the night."

"Where is she going?" asked Jenny, a puzzled look on her face.
Brad rolled his eyes. "Who the hell knows?"
Samantha grinned. "She's crazy."

"She's Chloe," replied Jake, smiling, defending his best friend. "You guys go on…I'll go find her."

"Well, hurry!" yelled Jeff. He looked at Brooke and smiled. "I've got things to do."

Jake took off running through the woods. He could hear the group's talking and laughter growing more distant as he made his way deeper into the forest. "Chloe! Where are you?" he yelled.

"Over here," her voice echoed from way in front of him.

"Get back over here, will you?" He finally spotted her in the midst of some trees.

"Catch me if you can!" she hollered back, laughing.

Jake rolled his eyes. "We haven't played that game in years, Chloe. Come on now!"

"You couldn't catch me then. I bet you still can't catch me! I'm too fast." She giggled.

Jake grinned. She *was* crazy. "You know I'll win. I always win."

"You suck!" she taunted.

Man, she was really asking for it! Jake's heart began to race. He laughed as he took off towards her. She playfully screamed when she saw him coming. In a flash, she was darting in and out of the trees, running as fast as she could. He ran fast too, catching glimpses of her as she disappeared and reappeared amongst the thick foliage. He was laughing, feeling like a kid again. It felt good to act silly, not to worry about anything. She had that way. She always knew how to make him smile. Jake pumped his legs harder. Damn, she was fast. She was swift like a deer, sailing over rocks and branches with ease. But Jake was fast too. Her laughter echoed in his ears and bounced off the surrounding landscape. It felt like they were the only two people in the world. He darted in a different direction, knowing that he would be able to cut her off. And then he spotted her just up ahead. She was smiling, her face glowing. She had no clue that he was this close. He ran up to her, surprising her as he swiftly grabbed her around the waist and swung her around. She laughed and screamed, amazed that he had caught up to her. He laughed too, feeling so exhilarated.

Jake stopped swinging her around and realized how good it felt to have her in his arms. He held on, looking at her in the moonlight. Some strands of her hair fell loose from her ponytail and graced her face, softening her look. She was out of breath from running. And so was he. She was looking at him too, something new flashing in her eyes. It made his heart skip a beat. She let him hold on to her a second longer. And then she pulled back and took his hand gently in hers.

"I want to show you something," she softly replied. He felt that familiar electricity shoot up his arm as she intertwined her fingers with his and led him through the trees. Even though he had felt it before, it never got old. It excited him more each time.

They came upon a glistening, natural lake, tucked away in the middle of nowhere. She let go of his hand and walked closer to it. Jake followed her, trying to control his pounding heart. He watched her as she gazed at the body of water. The moonlight reflected on its surface. "Isn't it the most beautiful thing you've ever seen?" she asked, breathlessly.

He let his eyes travel from her head all the way down her body. God, he could only imagine…"Yes, it is…" he whispered.

She turned to him, realizing he was looking at her, not the lake. Chloe smiled. She looked down and brushed past him. "Come on…we better get back."

Jake fought every urge to take Chloe in his arms and kiss her. She did something to him. He couldn't explain it. He took a deep breath, looked over his shoulder at the shimmering lake, knowing this was another special moment she was sharing with him. Another moment he would tuck away deep in that secret place in his mind.

"Are you coming?" she called from ahead of him.

Smiling to himself, he turned back around and ran to catch up to her.

Chapter 44

Chloe came home from school one day to find her father coming down the stairs with a suitcase. She stood there, shocked as hell to see him, blinking hard to make sure she wasn't dreaming. It had been months. She was too dumbfounded to ask him where he had been or what he had been doing.

He still looked like hell with sunken in eyes and a drawn up face.

"Daddy. What are you doing?" she managed to ask him.

"I came back to get the rest of my stuff." His voice was gruff and cold.

Chloe swallowed hard. Seeing him again took her back to that place. That place of fear and sadness. "Where are you going?"

"It doesn't matter." He stared at her, looking through her, just like he always did. Bill Mayer was still dead and empty inside. "I put the house in your name. You do what you want with it."

Chloe couldn't believe this. He was leaving for good. Forever. He brushed past her, carrying the suitcase. She whirled around. "I'm sorry, Daddy!" she blurted out. It was her final attempt at letting him know how she felt, how she hated the way life had turned out for the both of them, how she wished things could have been different.

He stopped dead in his tracks. Slowly, he turned and faced her. With a look of pure disgust, he grunted. "You should know this, Chloe." His hollow eyes narrowed. "You were an accident. I never wanted you. And if it weren't for you, she'd still be alive today." With that, he turned back around and walked out.

Sticks and stones may break my bones but words can never hurt me. Chloe always hated that saying and never believed it. But this time, surprisingly, as she watched her father pull away and drive off, she didn't shed a tear. Even as his haunting words echoed over and over in her mind, she managed to hold herself together. She just simply stared out the window and watched his car drive down the street until she couldn't see him anymore.

And when he was gone, she let her eyes focus on her own image that reflected back from the window. What stared back at her was a person who, no matter how hard she tried, couldn't make her mommy and daddy love her. What stared back at her was person who cried a lot through the years, who got into fights, who had nightmares, and who sunk down into the deepest depths of despair. *Haven't you ever dreamed about becoming someone different?* Samantha's words reverberated in her mind. Chloe focused on her reflection again. *Hell yeah.* She didn't want to be that person staring back at her anymore. It was time to let her go. It was time to start over and become someone new.

Chloe picked up the phone and dialed Samantha's number. When she heard Samantha answer, she smiled into the phone. "Hey, Sam! Do you and the girls feel like coming over and playing dress up tonight?"

Chapter 45

    Chloe was never more nervous in her life. It took three beers and a shot of tequila before the girls were able to talk her into coming. And now they were pulling up to the biggest party yet at "The Hills". Several of the surrounding high schools were here, forming one huge conglomerate rave. A DJ was pumping out electrifying music through huge speakers that everyone gyrated to. Four huge bonfires blazed, lighting up the night sky. It was definitely the place to be.
    Chloe swallowed hard as she and the girls got out of the vehicle. She stood there, unable to move forward. The girls all turned around. "Come on, Chloe! It's going to be so much fun!" they all hollered. She could see the excitement in their eyes. Chloe gave them a nervous smile. Tonight was a new beginning. It was time to see what this new beginning was going to bring.
    Chloe stepped forward and followed them towards the crowds. She wasn't sure how they would take her; how everyone would react. And then she started to notice….they were all turning, watching her as she walked by, taking a few seconds to recognize her. The girls looked at her with amazement, eyeing her from head to toe, giving her grins of approval. And the guys? Wow! The guys were all smiling, checking her out, taking her all in with their eyes.

She felt so different, so good…so beautiful. She wasn't that weird little girl anymore that everyone whispered horrible things about and avoided. They were coming up to her, talking to her, smiling at her, treating her like one of their own. Everywhere she went, guys were offering her drinks, wanting to stand by her side, competing for a moment of her time. They were doing anything to be with her. Chloe's heart thudded. She never knew it could be like this. That she could have this type of effect on people. It was amazing.

She took a bottle of beer someone offered to her. After taking a long drink from it, she stared into the bonfire. Yeah, tonight…tonight was going to be the beginning of Chloe's new life. She took another drink and then smiled.

Chapter 46

"You better slow down, Jeff. The night is still young," warned Jake. He stared at his crazy friend with the blond hair and blue eyes who was slamming his fifth beer.

"I'm feeling good, man. Tonight, this is my world…" Jeff held his arms open towards the hundreds of kids dancing. "And I'm going to conquer it all!"

Brad laughed, hollering in agreement. Yeah, they all felt good right now. They were all ready to party. Pretty girls were beginning to circle them like a school of shark. And the guys were more than willing to be their prey.

"Damn, there are a lot of hot girls here tonight," replied Brad, shaking his head and watching a girl walk by. He smiled after her, his classic good looks catching her eye in no time.

Jake laughed. His friends were a bad influence on him, but he liked it. Tonight, for him, it was no holds barred. He wanted to let loose too. There was something in the air. He could feel it.

Jeff whistled low, making Brad and Jake turn to him. "Now who is that sweet honey over there? Damn, she is smokin'!"

"Where!?" both Jake and Brad piped up like two horny school boys.

Jeff pointed towards one of the bonfires. "Over there, the one that has all the guys around her drooling like lovesick puppies."

Jake and Brad looked over at the girl Jeff was pointing out. Her back was to them, so they couldn't see her face. All of them drew in their breaths. She had long brown hair, a tight black vest like top and even tighter jeans that accentuated her backside like they had never seen. She was slender, toned, athletic looking. The three guys stared over at her, gazing at her body that just wouldn't quit.

"Damn, she is hot..." replied Jake under his breath. And then the girl turned where they could barely see the side of her face. She held a bottle of beer up to her mouth and took a drink. She stared off into the fire again, oblivious to all the looks she was getting. Jake frowned. She seemed awfully familiar. He strained his eyes harder. And then his eyes grew to the size of grapefruits. "Holy shit!!" he exclaimed.

"What?" Jeff and Brad asked in unison, not taking their eyes away from this mysterious, sexy girl.

Jake's heart thudded. "That's Chloe!"

"What!?" they both exclaimed again in unison. They all strained their eyes this time, not believing what they were seeing.

"Jesus," breathed Brad. "That *is* Chloe!" She was holding and drinking her beer just like the old Chloe did.

"Oh my god," replied Jeff, unable to tear his eyes away from her, just as his friends couldn't either.

And right then, they saw Chloe happen to glance over at them. A huge smile spread across her lips. She began to stroll over to them, making all the guys' heads turn as she walked. Big loop earrings bounced as she sexily swung her long, silky hair over her bare shoulder. Red lipstick on full lips contrasted against her porcelain skin and long, dark eyelashes batted up against her cheeks. Full breasts peeked up over her V-neck top that hugged every inch of her long curves. Years of being a full blown athletic tomboy paid off as they stared at her rock hard abs that were fully exposed by her low cut, tight as sin blue jeans. Her legs were long and lean and her curvy hips swayed effortlessly as she walked in high heeled designer boots.

She didn't look like an 18 year old high school girl. She looked like a model…a goddess…a…

"Hi, fellas," she casually replied when she came up upon them. They couldn't stop staring, their jaws open in total shock. Up and down, all around. She was all woman. All beautiful. All sexy as hell. And all these years, they never had a clue that she was hiding all of that underneath it all…

Chloe grinned. "Well….what do you think?" She knew she had them completely enthralled with her.

Jeff stared at her breasts. "I think you look hot as hell!"

Brad immediately nudged him, embarrassed by his brash comment.

Chloe grinned.

Jake cleared his throat. "I think what Jeff is trying to say is…" He gave Jeff a look of warning and then looked back at Chloe, grinning. "…that it's a good look for you." They couldn't tear their eyes away. It was unbelievable that this was Chloe standing in front of them.

Chloe looked down, grinning. "Well…that's good to know." She gave Jake her beer bottle, brushed past them and walked towards her group of girlfriends who were all waiting for her, smiling from ear to ear. They were obviously thrilled with the reaction Chloe was getting out of the guys.

Jake, Jeff and Brad let their eyes follow Chloe as she walked away, taking in every inch of her, shaking their heads in awe at her amazing transformation.

Jake grinned. He didn't know what was going on with Chloe, but he liked it. There *was* something in the air tonight. He had a feeling things were about to get a little crazy.

Chapter 47

"They can't stop looking at you! *Jake* can't stop looking at you!" whispered Samantha. She had the hugest smile on her face. "He thinks you are so hot!" She and Chloe stood next to each other with their other girlfriends surrounding them.

"Do you really think so?" asked Chloe. She laughed, glancing over at the guys. Amidst all the girls coming up to them, vying for their attention, she could see that they were watching her, trying to be discreet about it, whispering to each other.

"How does that make you feel?" asked Samantha. Her eyes were sparkling. She was so happy for her friend.

Chloe was nervous. "I don't know. Kind of scared."

Samantha raised her eyebrow. "You should make a move."

Chloe shook her head. "I don't know if I can do that."

Samantha laughed. "Chloe! Look at him! He is so unbelievably gorgeous. Every girl at this party is wanting him right now. You've got to make a move!"

Chloe felt so awkward. This was Jake they were talking about. Her best friend. She had grown up with him. How was she supposed to make a move?

She stole a glance over at him. Samantha was right. He *was* gorgeous with his dark hair and dark eyes. He was so tall and strong with an amazing smile. Just looking at him now made the butterflies in her stomach flutter like crazy. "Maybe I should wait for him to make a move." Chloe couldn't believe she was even talking about this.

Samantha frowned and nodded in disagreement. "He's got girls all over him right now. He's not going to. Besides, he respects you too much."

"He makes moves on girls all the time."

Samantha gave Chloe a knowing look.

Chloe laughed. "Ok, ok. I'll quit talking about those other girls." She stole another glance at Jake. He was stealing a glance at her too, playing it cool so the other girls around him wouldn't notice. Chloe quickly looked away. Just knowing that she had turned his head with her new image made her extremely nervous. "Give me another beer or this is going to be a long night." She slammed her 4th bottle of confidence, wishing her heart would stop pounding so hard.

After ten minutes, the buzz in Chloe's head started to feel really good. Her inhibitions were starting to disappear. She was relaxing more. She could tell her girlfriends were too. Guys were coming up to them now, asking her and the girls to dance. Chloe had never been one to dance much but she told herself this was a step towards leaving the old Chloe behind. She gladly accepted.

The good looking guy took her hand. Chloe looked around. Her friends were all about her, letting loose, having fun, dancing. Chloe listened to the pulsating music and saw the look of admiration in the guy's eyes. He was captivated by her beauty. It shocked her at first. But then, something inside of her came alive. She realized that he wanted her. They *all* wanted her. That fact made her feel sexy and desirable. Chloe let the alcohol and the music take over. She forgot about everything around her and began dancing, moving her body, slowly realizing that it was coming naturally. The more she moved, the more his eyes drank her in. He inched closer, putting his hands on her body, making her feel amazing. She had him in the palm of her hand. And she knew that at that moment, he would have done anything for her. In the midst of it all, she glanced over at the Brad,

Jeff and Jake. They were watching with looks in their eyes she had only seen them give to other girls. Especially Jake. His eyes burned with an intensity she had never seen before. The questions began bombarding her mind. Was she really having an effect on him? Did he really want her? Was he excited as she was about all of this? She just didn't know.

Chapter 48

Jake smiled at the girl who was talking to him. He wasn't hearing a thing she was saying, though, but he was sure good at pretending. Out of the corner of his eye, he was watching *her*. She was amazing, breathtaking, unbelievable. My God, that was Chloe out there, taking everybody's breath away. She was dancing, smiling and looking like she was having the time of her life. He had never seen her look like that. She literally glowed.

"So Jake, what are you drinking tonight?" someone was asking him.

"What?" He snapped back out of his trance. Pretty girls were all around him, talking to him, giving him those looks he knew too well. But none of them, absolutely none of them held a candle to *her*. Jake made small talk, being polite, playing along to keep them happy as he continued to steal glances at Chloe. He watched her drop dead gorgeous body move, feeling something inside of him begin to stir. It had always been there, hidden deep inside because he had purposely suppressed it. But seeing her tonight so sexy and alive made him feel alive too. His stomach was doing flip flops and his heart was pounding. Like every other guy here, he wanted to be with her. But for him, it ran deeper than that. He couldn't explain it.

Jake looked over at his buddies. They too were entranced with Chloe. She had been their good friend since sixth grade. "Just one of the guys" as they had always put it. Chloe could hang just as tough as any guy they knew. No doubt about it. But now, here she was, completely out of her element, shocking them, making them realize she wasn't just one of the guys anymore. She was a whole lot more than any of them ever suspected.

The song that was playing ended and Jake, Brad and Jeff casually watched as Chloe and her girlfriends made their way back to where they were all hanging out. Jake was so unbelievably nervous. That was so unlike him. He was never shy when it came to hooking up with girls. But this wasn't just any girl. This was Chloe. Jake fidgeted, trying to play it cool with the girls that were around him, Brad and Jeff. He racked his brain, trying to think of an excuse to go over there.

Without even realizing it, Brad read his mind. "If you ladies will excuse us, we've got some friends over there we'd like to say hi to." They politely ducked out and headed over to Chloe and her friends. Being the ladies man that he was, Brad smiled as they walked up. "Hello ladies. We couldn't help but notice all the attention you all were stirring up. So we just had to come over here and see what was going on." He glanced at Chloe, looking her up and down.

She blushed and looked away, smiling nonetheless. Everyone began talking and mingling. Jake tried to remain calm. He continued to play it cool, keeping his distance from Chloe, trying to figure out what to do next. God, this was absolutely crazy. He was so nervous. He took a swallow from his bottle, hoping to gain a little more courage from the alcohol. He stole a quick glance. Wow, she was just so pretty. *Ok, quick...look away! Try not to look so desperate. You're such an ass, Jake! Chloe's your best friend. She trusts you! How can you look at her that way?* He stole another glance. *Man, her hair is so long. Her body...my God, that body. What the hell is wrong with you! Stop it! Look away! In fact, quit looking all together. Get it out of your mind!*

"Are you ok, Jake?"

THE DIAMOND HILLS

He turned to see Chloe standing in front of him, a concerned look on her beautiful face. "Yeah, I'm fine." He hoped she didn't hear his voice crack.

She smiled at him, sending chills down his spine. "You look...disturbed."

He raised an eyebrow. "Disturbed?"

She laughed. He must have had a funny look on his face. "Yeah..."

He laughed too, feeling a little less nervous.

"Are you having fun tonight?" she asked.

He nodded casually. "Yeah, are you?"

She nodded too. "I am." She leaned in. "I was just so nervous showing up here tonight like this. It's so...different for me."

She was confiding in him again. Just like always. It made him feel good. He could tell it made her feel good too. "You don't have to be nervous, Chloe." He stole a quick glance at her tiny waist and her curvy hips. She was so petite. "You look great." There. He said it. And he meant it.

Chloe grinned, her eyes sparkling. "Thanks. It means a lot that you think so."

She was doing it again. Making him feel like he was the only thing that mattered. She always had that way.

A popular, upbeat song began blaring through the speakers. Kids hollered and rushed out to dance with one another. Brad came up, grinning. "Chloe, you gonna stand here all night or you gonna dance with me?" Before she could answer, he was taking her hand. Jake's heart sank. He didn't want her to go. He was enjoying this.

Chloe must have read his mind. She grinned and linked her left arm with Jake's right arm, dragging him with her and Brad. "Come on, Jake!"

Jake was shocked. He didn't know what was going on. But at that point, he didn't care. He followed Chloe and Brad out to where people were gyrating to the sexy rhythm. Brad took the lead, pulling Chloe close, swaying with her, placing his hands on her hips. She in turn, put one hand on his shoulder and with the other, pulled Jake close until his body was pressed behind her. Chloe was in the middle, sandwiched between Jake and Brad. Jake's heart thudded hard in his chest. He was touching her, feeling her body against his as she moved seductively. She was throwing her head back against his shoulder, holding on to him while holding on to Brad too. They began to draw attention.

"Damn!" he heard Jeff say. "I'm getting in on some of that!" Jeff walked up with Brooke. Pretty soon, Jake felt Brooke's body pressed up against his as Jeff pushed his body up against Brooke's. Jenny came up behind Brad, rubbing her hands up and down his chest and stomach. And then another guy came up behind Jenny and another guy came up behind Brooke. And so it went. One guy and one girl. They all formed one long seductive line, gyrating with each other, turning each other on, not caring who was watching. And everyone was watching.

Jake's body was on fire. His head was spinning, partly from alcohol and partly from the fact that hands were all over him, touching him, turning him on. Through the lustful fog in his eyes, he watched Brad and Chloe dancing with each other, touching each other's bodies. He couldn't believe this was happening. It was crazy, sexy, erotic. He loved it. He loved feeling this way, so alive and carefree. He loved feeling Chloe pushed up against him. Her body was so close, stirring those feelings deep inside of him. He reached down, placing his hands on her hips and letting them travel to her stomach, holding her even closer to him. She arched her back and placed her head on his shoulder, leaning her face close to his. He let his lips graze her bare shoulders. He could smell the sexy scent of her perfume. She turned around to face him. Her eyes held something he had never seen before. They were full of lust, passion, seductiveness.

Jake ran his hands down her bare arms, feeling her hips sway. She wrapped her arms around his neck, holding him close. Their faces were just inches away from each others. He had never been more turned on than he was right then. He wanted to grab her, kiss her, rub her all over. Jake forgot about everyone else around them.

He focused only on Chloe. In his mind, she was with him and only him.

Brad must have sensed the chemistry between the two of them. He backed off and turned around to focus on Jenny. Chloe was grinning at Jake. He could tell she was having the time of her life, daring to act like no one she had ever acted like before. He liked it. He looked in her eyes. She grew serious, focusing on his lips. Did she want him to kiss her? His heart thudded uncontrollably. He didn't know what to do. As excited as he was, he was scared to death. They had never been this far before. They had never let it get to this point. And now, they were on the brink of falling over the edge.

Jake felt the heat from her body overtaking him. He felt himself becoming extremely aroused, embarrassed by it, hoping she couldn't tell. But she was driving him crazy. Like no one else ever had. They stopped swaying, holding each other, staring into each other's eyes. His lips were mere millimeters from hers.

"Jake..." she whispered breathlessly.

Jake closed his eyes. He couldn't stop. This was it. This was what he had been waiting so long for....

"The cops, everyone! 5-0 just pulled up!" shouted the DJ into the mike. Jake's eyes flew open. Everyone was scattering like cockroaches, running like crazy in every direction. They could hear the sirens now and screeching tires. Jake and Chloe quickly pulled apart, caught up in the chaos. Brad and Jeff were taking off in one direction. Jake snapped back to reality. He grabbed Chloe's hand.

"Come on!" he shouted to her, dragging her off towards his pickup. They made a mad dash towards the vehicle and jumped in. Jake quickly put the truck in gear and spun out as he pushed hard on the accelerator, weaving in and out of all the other cars around him that were trying to do the same thing. They somehow made it past everyone, skidding onto a dirt road only to find a cop car hot on their trail. Sirens blared and lights flashed. "Shit!" shouted Jake. He had no intentions of getting caught.

He sped up, bouncing over bumps and rocks as they flew through the forest. The cop car was close behind. Chloe looked over her shoulder. Her eyes were wide with excitement. She seemed to be enjoying the chase. Her hair whipped around her wildly. Jake glanced over at her. God she was beautiful, sitting there, looking just like that. And then she grinned at him. Her eyes sparkled with an animalistic craziness. "Faster, Jake! Go faster!"

For a split second, Jake was seven again, playing with Chloe on the school's merry go round. He saw her laying flat on her back towards the middle. He was running alongside it, pushing it as hard as he could, only to hear her telling him, "Faster Jake! Go faster!" They were so young, trying their best to be innocent little kids in a horrible big world. Memories like that became compartmentalized in the back of his mind until moments like this brought them back out. Jake smiled at her. That little girl on the playground had grown up to be such a gorgeous young lady. And that gorgeous young lady was now sitting in his truck. She was still Chloe. Still his one and only Chloe who made him feel invincible, believing in him and knowing that he could go faster. Jake pushed the accelerator all the way to the floor, swerving the truck dangerously back and forth.

Chloe hollered with excitement. She looked over her shoulder again. Jake looked in his rearview mirror to see a huge cloud of dust. Jake quickly turned the wheel sharp, making them skid towards the right. They came dangerously close to losing control. But it didn't even phase Chloe. She laughed, throwing her pretty head back, running her hands through her long hair. Jake laughed too, feeling his adrenaline pumping hard through his body. They cut off through the woods on another dirt road, quickly losing the cops. Chloe leaned out the window. "See you, suckers!" she shouted. Jake laughed out loud at her boldness. Before long they were heading back into town. Chloe seemed like she was on a natural high. He slowed down, his hands shaking on the steering wheel.

"Oh, that was so fun!" she exclaimed. She grinned at him. "Tell me we can do that again sometime…" Her eyes shone with excitement.

He shook his head yes. He glanced at her out of the corner of his eye. She was grinning from ear to ear, looking out the window. She seemed so happy, this new Chloe. It was so good to see her this happy.

They drove in silence the few minutes it took to reach Chloe's house. Jake turned the pickup off. They both sat there, wondering what to do next. Jake awkwardly turned to look at her. God, she looked so good, half hidden in the shadows of his pickup. She glanced at him nervously, searching for something to say too. Finally Jake spoke up. "Chloe, I had such a good time tonight."

She smiled at him. "Me too. It was unbelievable."

Jake looked at her red lips. His heart thudded again. Earlier, he had been so close to kissing her. And now, he wanted nothing more than to try again. She sensed his intentions. They both leaned in, slowly. Jake closed his eyes, ready to do it this time.

A horn blared from behind them and tires screeched loudly as another pickup came to a sudden stop beside them. Chloe and Jake looked out Jake's window, startled.

"Dude! Did you see how many cops were back there?" shouted a drunk Jeff as he leaned lazily out the passenger side window. He, Brooke, Jenny and Brad were all in Brad's pickup.

"Hi Chloe!" the girls responded in unison.

Chloe raised her hand and waved hello.

"That was crazy! It was like cops and robbers back there," exclaimed Brad. He took a swig from his beer bottle. With the other hand, he casually draped it around Jenny's shoulders. The girls were giggling and music was blaring from inside the cab. They were all obviously high strung.

Jake tried to hide his disappointment in being interrupted for the second time. "Yeah, they chased us for a while but we managed to lose them."

"Those losers can never catch us!" hollered Jeff. He whooped like a mad man, making Brooke laugh.

"We're going to another party at Carson's house. You guys wanna come along?" asked Brad.

Jake quickly looked at Chloe and then back at the guys. "No, I think I'm going to turn in." He just wanted to be left alone. He just wanted some quiet time with Chloe.

His answer did not get a good response from his friends. They groaned with disappointment, egging him on to come along.

Chloe smiled. She reached over and squeezed Jake's hand. "Goodnight," she told him. She quickly got out of the pickup before Jake had a chance to say anything.

Jake wanted to stop her. But he didn't want to make a scene in front of everybody.

"Goodnight, Chloe! See you later. We'll see you Monday at school," all her friends shouted after her. She told them goodbye and walked up to her house.

Jake watched her disappear through the front door, wishing he could go after her. But he realized this was something he had to be real careful with. It was all so strange for the both of them. Exhilarating, but scary as hell. He knew she was feeling it too. Jake told his friends goodbye as they peeled out and headed off into the night. Jake looked back towards Chloe's house one last time. He started his truck up, sighed, and headed home.

Chapter 49

Jake finished toweling off and got dressed. He listened to his buddies talking about their crazy weekend with the girls they hooked up with. The boys' locker room was infamous for exchanging stories about hot girls and great lays. Funny, Jake was never one to divulge his conquests. It just wasn't him, much to the other guys' dismay. The three friends headed towards the main building to get to their next class. They walked down the hall, dodging other students.

"So, Jake. Did anything ever happen with you and Chloe this weekend?" asked Brad.

Jake shook his head. "Nah. We both had to work. I haven't even seen her." He cleared his throat, obviously uncomfortable discussing it. They turned down another hall and saw Chloe in the distance, talking to some guys that were overtly admiring her new look. She was beautiful. Brad, Jeff and Jake stopped, watching her as she smiled and laughed at whatever the guys were telling her.

Jeff spoke up. "So is anything *going* to happen with you and Chloe?" He grinned, nudging Jake.

Without taking his eyes from her, Jake spoke. "I don't know. Should it?"

Brad put his hand on Jake's shoulder. "Dude, look at her." They all stared in silence for a few seconds longer. "Forget the fact that she is unbelievably hot. Chloe's like…the greatest girl in the world."

Jeff shook his head in agreement. "Yeah, I'd go after her myself." Then he turned to Jake. "But I'm not the one she's interested in." He patted Jake on the back and he and Brad left for class, leaving Jake standing there, soaking in what they had just told him. Chloe turned then and caught his eye. She smiled at him and waved. He waved back, giving her an awkward smile. He turned and headed to class.

Chapter 50

As soon as she walked in, Chloe locked all the doors and checked all the windows. It was routine, even in broad daylight. She didn't want to be like that but she had no choice. They had made her that way. Her dead mother that haunted her dreams at night. Her abusive father whom she feared would show up out of the blue one day to beat her up again. And Ty. The boy she thought she could fall for who nearly raped her of her innocence. It was horrible hiding this part of her. Even though she was trying to open up, trying to become a different person, deep down inside, she was still broken. She wondered if she'd ever be able to put all the pieces back together.

It had been busy tonight at the restaurant. But thank God for her job. She was surviving, paying the bills, buying food and clothes. Chloe grunted. Here she was, barely 18 and completely on her own. She had no one to turn to for parental support, emotionally or financially. If it weren't for Jake, she would truly be alone in this world.

Chloe ate something quick, sat down at the kitchen table and began going through the bills, figuring out which ones she could pay and which ones would have to wait until her next paycheck. And then she hit the books, working on her homework. It was late by the time she finally crawled into bed. She laid there for a long time, her mind racing. So much was weighing on her conscience. Sleep continued to be elusive. She thought of school, work, college and of course, Jake.

He didn't know how much she thought of him over the last several years. Chloe smiled in the dark, recalling the exact moment she realized she had grown attracted to Jake. It was the summer they were both 13, lying on their backs side by side underneath the stars at their secret hiding place. He was telling her about some baseball game he had seen on T.V. She watched him talk, suddenly seeing him in a whole new light. They were both changing, growing up. Jake's maturing voice cracked as he spoke, making her smile even more. Just being with him put her on top of the world.

And from there her secret attraction continued to grow. But Chloe was a tomboy. She didn't wear fancy designer clothes that the other girls at the junior high were starting to wear, nor did she spend hours styling her hair. And Jake? Well, Chloe could see he was starting to look at girls like that. Secretly, when he didn't think she was looking, he would steal second glances at these girls as they walked by. That's what he liked. And Chloe was so different from girls like that. She could throw mean curveballs and even meaner punches.

So Chloe hid her growing interest in Jake, feeling foolish about it all. She resigned herself to the fact that it was just better if Jake and she remained best friends. Being just friends was much easier anyway.

But now, as Chloe lay in the dark, thinking of Jake's dark, piercing eyes and captivating smile, her heart began to flutter. Things weren't so easy or simplistic anymore. Things were changing. He was looking at her in a whole new way, making her pulse race and her body tremble. They weren't prepubescent teens anymore. They were becoming young adults on the verge of stepping out into a whole new world. Chloe wasn't sure what that meant for Jake and her. What was going to happen to them? They had always had each other. Soon, they would be going their separate ways for the first time. And in the midst of all this uncertainty, new feelings were surfacing. Feelings that scared Chloe to death yet excited her at the same time. Was it the right thing to do? To let themselves venture to a place they had always felt was forbidden? What would they find there? Love and passion? Or hurt and regret? These conflicting thoughts are what tore at Chloe. Jake was her everything. She couldn't lose him. But the more time she spent with him, the more tempted she was to take the risk. Her secret attraction to him was surfacing now and she found it harder to suppress, especially when she knew he was growing attracted to her too.

Chloe sighed and turned to her side. She closed her eyes, trying to let sleep overtake her, knowing she would probably be awakened by another nightmare. These were new nightmares. Nightmares of Ty and other unknown men who attacked her, trying to make her succumb to their evil advances. Chloe opened her eyes and frowned. Why did Ty have to mess her up like that? Wasn't she messed up enough already? She would wake up terrified, searching frantically around her dark room for their shadows, praying each time that she wouldn't find them really standing there.

Chloe swallowed hard now, anticipating the fear that overtook her on a nightly basis. She rubbed her head that was beginning to throb. God, she hated all these shattered fragments in her mind. Even now, she still felt on the brink of losing it. Was this what her mother went through before she went over the edge? She thought of her mother and then she thought of her father's final words. They haunted her now, eating at her, making her crazy all over again. Chloe covered her face with her hands, wishing there was a way she could make it all stop. And then she remembered what Jake had told her. Chloe sighed deeply, closing her eyes. She found Jake in the far recesses of her mind. He was waiting for her there with open arms that always kept her safe. She snuggled into them, listening to his heart. He rocked her gently back and forth until she fell asleep.

Chapter 51

Jake was excited. But as always, he played it cool. Brad and Jeff didn't have a clue. Or at least he hoped they didn't. They pulled up to her house, idling by the curb. It was Saturday night and they were waiting to pick Chloe up. Jake hadn't seen much of her all week, only between classes here and there. They both stayed extremely busy with school and work. But tonight, he hoped, would be an opportunity to spend some time with her.

She bounded out the front door and down the walk. The boys stared at her. She looked amazing with her styled hair and her form fitting, button down top and tight jeans. Even seeing her now, they still couldn't get over that this was the Chloe they had all grown up with. She gave them all a killer smile.

Brad hopped out, holding the door for her, unable to keep himself from checking out her back side as she climbed in the pickup. He smiled approvingly to himself. He got in, sandwiching Chloe between him and Jake.

Jeff, who was sitting behind them, reached over and hugged Chloe around the shoulders. Jeff had always been the most openly affectionate guy of the group, but alcohol made it even more prevalent. "Hi, Chloe," he slurred, already well on his way to becoming completely inebriated. He kissed her on the top of the head.

Chloe didn't seem to mind. She laughed it off, knowing that Jeff was just being Jeff. He was harmless.

"Alright! Let's go party, people!" shouted Jeff. Jake put the pickup in gear and they headed off.

Jake's heart was thudding again. Just feeling her next to him was driving him crazy. He wanted so badly to reach down and take her hand. Was she feeling it too? He couldn't tell. She just seemed to glow, being with all of them. They seemed to truly make her happy.

"So Jeff, you gonna share any of your liquor with the rest of us?" asked Jake, looking in his rearview mirror.

Jeff bent down and clanked some bottles around. "Shit," he said.

Brad groaned. "Don't tell me you drank all of that in the time it took us to drive from your house to Chloe's!"

"I was thirsty, man!" Jeff tried to defend himself.

They all hollered disapprovingly at him.

"Well, I guess we're going to have to make a pit stop," replied Jake as he turned off the main highway. They headed towards the one liquor store where they knew the owner would sell to them. Pulling up into the parking lot, they all groaned again.

"Damn it! Ralph's working tonight!" exclaimed Brad. Ralph was the owner's employee. He hated Jake and the guys and therefore refused to sell to them no matter how much they tried to bribe him.

Jake shut the pickup off and turned to Chloe. "Alright, Chloe. You know what to do."

Chloe groaned. "No! You know he gives me the creeps."

"He likes you, Chloe," replied Jake matter-of-factly. It was no secret that Ralph had the biggest crush on her. The usual stubborn as a mule Ralph turned into a real pushover if Chloe was around.

Jeff leaned forward. "Yeah, especially now…maybe he'll sell you the whole store."

Chloe frowned. "I hate doing this." She crossed her arms in front of her chest.

"Do you want alcohol or not? Look at Jeff. He's suffering from withdrawals already." Jake pointed to Jeff. Brad laughed out loud.

Chloe frowned even more. "I hate you guys!"

Jeff wrapped his arms around Chloe's shoulders again. "You love us and you know it."

She shoved him off. "Get off of me and Annie up." She extended her hand as they all shoved their share of money into it. Brad laughed again as he let her out. She didn't seem too thrilled about having to flirt with Ralph just so they could buy alcohol.

The guys watched Chloe walk across the parking lot. "We shouldn't be looking at her like this," replied Jake, not taking his eyes from her.

"Yeah, you're probably right," said Brad. But neither he nor Jeff could tear their eyes away from her either.

Jeff leaned out the window and shouted, "Shake it a little more, Chloe and maybe he'll throw in a bottle of Jack!" Brad and Jeff laughed. Jake grinned. Chloe turned around and flipped them all the bird, a dirty look on her pretty face. She turned back around and sexily sauntered up to the door, assuming the role she knew she had to play. The guys all watched carefully.

Through the huge glass windows of the liquor store, they could see Ralph looking at a paper, his feet propped up on the counter, oblivious to who had just walked in. Chloe slowly and sexily walked up and propped her elbows on the counter, sticking her hips and butt out behind her.

Jake laughed. "Holy shit! She's really milking this, isn't she?"

Brad grinned. "Hell yeah, she is!"

Jeff's eyes gleamed as he continued to watch.

Chloe must have said something. Ralph lowered his paper. When he saw who it was, he dropped his paper and nearly fell off of his stool. Brad, Jeff and Jake laughed out loud as they watched Ralph stumble clumsily back onto his feet, his big beer belly jiggling in front of him. Even from where they were sitting, they could see how nervous and excited Ralph was to see Chloe, especially with her new, sexy look.

Chloe remained calm and collected, playing the part like a true pro. She was smiling at him, making small talk, batting her eyelashes. He walked out from behind the counter, standing closer to her. She stood up and walked to the back of the store; Ralph following close behind, staring at her backside. She continued to flirt with him as she opened up the glass refrigerator doors that housed the liquor and began grabbing beer. He even helped her carry some back up to the front.

Jake shook his head, smiling. She was absolutely amazing.

She proceeded to check out. At the last minute, she leaned in and whispered something into his ear, touching his arm as she spoke. Ralph grinned nervously. He walked to a nearby shelf and picked up a bottle of whiskey.

Jeff laughed. "She's awesome!"

They watched as Ralph walked back behind the counter and slipped the bottle into the brown sack. He put his fingers up to his lips, telling her to keep it a secret. Chloe smiled sexily at him and paid. Ralph's eyes stayed glued onto her until she was out of the store. Chloe walked back across the parking lot, holding the liquor up in triumph, smiling from ear to ear.

The boys whooped and hollered. She ran up to the vehicle and got in. They all laughed, cheering her on. She began distributing the liquor. "You guys owe me big time for that one!" She looked at Jake out of the corner of her eye and grinned. He grinned back at her. "Now give me one of those so I can forget about what I just had to do to get it." She laughed out loud, taking a long drink from her bottle. Jake started up his pickup and they headed back out towards the main drag.

Ten minutes later, they were all feeling pretty good. Loud music blared from Jake's speakers. They were all joking, having a good time. Just then, a black SUV pulled up along side them with about five guys in it. Jake recognized them. They were a bunch of hotshot trouble makers from a nearby high school. He hadn't seen them in awhile.

The driver leaned out his window. He was cocky and arrogant. "Feel like racing that piece of shit tonight, boys? That is, if your chick there doesn't mind."

They didn't recognize Chloe. Brad shook his head. "Go race on your own streets, Branson. You know you can't hang."

Caleb Branson grimaced. "What are you, a bunch of pussies?!"

"Screw you!" hollered Jeff.

Jake shouted at him. "You wanna race? We'll race, just to watch you lose!"

"We'll see about that!" he shouted back. Both he and Jake accelerated. Chloe rolled her eyes. Jake knew she hated those guys. They were a bunch of assholes always trying to cause trouble. Jake and Caleb ran neck and neck, dangerously careening down the street. The pickup began to shake as Jake sped up. He wanted to teach those guys a lesson.

"Alright. This is bullshit," commented Chloe. She began unbuttoning her top. Jake and the guys stared at her.

"What the hell are you doing?" exclaimed Jake, trying to keep his hands on the steering wheel while his eyes bounced from the road back to her full breasts that swelled above her lace bra.

Chloe crawled over Brad's legs and leaned all the way out the window, her hair blowing wildly around.

"Hey, Caleb!" she shouted.

Caleb Branson pulled his eyes away from the road and turned, along with the other guys in the SUV.

"Can I catch a ride?" she coyly replied, smiling and letting them take in every inch of her plunging cleavage.

Caleb's eyes grew huge as instant recognition hit him square in the face. "Chloe?!" he squealed, his voice cracking. The shock of seeing her like that made him swerve. In a split second, he was braking hard, trying to keep from losing control. Too late. Chloe and the guys watched as the SUV spun a couple of times before coming to a complete stop in the middle of the road.

She climbed back in, buttoning up her top. The guys laughed and looked at her in amazement.

Jeff fell back against the seat. "Ok, I'm going to be back here jacking off now."

Brad and Jake laughed so hard they thought they might cry. Chloe simply smiled to herself. She looked at Jake and gestured towards her chest. "I'm quickly finding out that these things are becoming pretty handy!"

"You're crazy, Chloe Mayer," he told her.

She didn't say another word.

Chapter 52

Her heart skipped a beat when she saw them coming. She couldn't help it. She had told herself months ago that she was over it and that she had finally moved on. But deep down inside, she still wondered why he didn't fall for her.

Molly Watters had kept a low profile, staying out of the party scene, keeping away from "The Diamond Hills", specifically to avoid him. He had broken her heart, had completely torn it to shreds. Did he even know it? Did he even care?

So tonight, after months of lying low, she let her friends talk her into coming out again. Only to see him. What luck. She stared from across the way, watching their shadows move closer. He was hotter than ever, turning heads as he walked. Brad and Jeff did the same, so good looking that they didn't even realize it. But something was different. Chloe. My God, look at Chloe. Molly almost didn't recognize her. Where had she been hiding? Molly never saw her at school. If she was stunning before, she was absolutely breathtaking now. And she walked in the middle of them, up front. Not behind them like she used to. Her head was held up high; she was smiling. *A different person.* Molly watched, mesmerized by her beauty. Her eyes followed her until she disappeared into the middle of a group of people.

Molly turned her attention back to Jake. He was walking by her now, realizing she was here. He stopped and smiled.

"Hello, Molly." His eyes held nothing. No fire. Not even a flickering ember. Molly did nothing for him.

She managed a weak smile. "Hi, Jake. What are you up to tonight?"

He shifted awkwardly from one foot to the other, looking around, looking everywhere. Everywhere but at her. "Just out with the guys." He cleared his throat. "And you? Haven't seen you in a while."

"I've been busy. School projects, cheerleading. You know…?" she lied. She should have told him that since he had pushed her away, she had spent every waking moment coming up with new and creative ways to avoid him, just as he had avoided her.

He shook his head. "Yeah, well….it was good seeing you."

Her heart pounded. He was so handsome. "It was good seeing you too." Her eyes followed him as he walked away. It felt like someone just stabbed a knife into her chest. She didn't realize how much it would hurt to run into him again. She stealthily watched as he made his way around, mingling. Girls flocked to him, vying for his attention. He was nice, smiling, chatting. But through it all, Molly noticed one thing. His eyes always wandered. When he thought no one was looking, he was gazing at Chloe. Looking at Chloe the way Molly always hoped he would look at her. Molly felt the knife go in deeper. But now she understood. She finally understood.

Molly waited for the right opportunity. She had to get it off her chest. It was eating her up inside. Chloe had wandered off. Molly found her standing alone away from the crowds. She seemed a million miles away, staring off towards the trees, just like the old Chloe used to do. Carefully she approached. Chloe turned, startled.

"Molly! You scared me," she replied, holding her hand over her heart.

"I'm sorry. Didn't mean to sneak up on you." She walked up, staring at Chloe in the dark, looking at her hair, her features, her body. She was so beautiful. She had always been so beautiful. Why couldn't she see it all before?

Chloe looked at her as if she was wondering why Molly was here.

Molly opened her mouth. "It was you."

Chloe looked puzzled. "Excuse me?"

Molly slowly shook her head. "For the last several months, I've beat myself up wondering why. Now I know."

Chloe continued to look puzzled.

"No matter how hard I would have tried, it wouldn't have mattered." She paused, taking in a deep breath. "He'll never love anyone else. Because it was always you." Molly stared deep into her eyes. "You're the one," she whispered. Tears began to sting her eyes. Damn it! She didn't want to lose it in front of Chloe. But it was just so heartbreaking.

Chloe looked genuinely upset. She reached out to touch her on the shoulder. "Molly…"

But Molly didn't let her say anymore. And she didn't let Chloe touch her. She just quickly turned around and walked away.

Chapter 53

Chloe closed her eyes, rubbing her forehead with her hand. That was not cool at all. She never liked to see anyone upset, especially that upset. Molly had been nice. She had been one of the few that had treated Chloe half way decently. And now, Chloe felt that Molly's unhappiness was somehow all her fault, even though she hadn't a clue why. Another screw up. Chalk it up with all the rest.

Chloe sighed and decided to head back to the party. She made her way through the crowds of kids. Looking up ahead, her heart suddenly leapt to her throat. She froze dead in her tracks, her body trembling and breaking out into a cold sweat.

Looking straight at her was Ty Snyder, his blue eyes burning a hole right through her. Jesus Christ. He had come back for her. To finish what he had started. Chloe blinked hard, hoping she was having one of her nightmares. But she was awake and he was still staring at her. She watched as he began making his way towards her.

Chloe felt the adrenaline in her body begin to surge. *No way! Not again!* He wasn't going to get her. She turned and tried to shove her way back through the crowds, hearing her heart in her ears. People were shouting at her, getting angry that she was pushing them out of the way. But he was hot on her trail. She could feel it. *Get away!*

Run as fast as you can! Get the hell out of here! He's going to get you, Chloe! In a panic, she began shoving more people out of the way, trying to make her rubbery legs move faster. At last she broke free from the crowds, ready to run when she felt someone grabbing her arm. Holy shit! It was him! He had her! He had her! She opened her mouth to scream…but nothing came out.

Chapter 54

"Chloe! Stop! Stop!" Jake shouted. She was trying to wrestle free, not seeing who he was, shoving him away from her. "It's me! Jake!"

She turned, her eyes wild with fear, suddenly recognizing who had a hold of her. She pulled her arm free, looking past Jake towards the crowds of people staring at her. Her eyes searched frantically around.

Jake shook his head. "It's not him, Chloe. It's not Ty." Jake had seen it all. He had watched from a distance as she tensed up with fear, knowing what was going through her mind. It scared him to see her that terrified. He realized then just how messed up she was over this. He reached out for her arm. "Just someone who looks like him. That's all."

Chloe shoved him off, embarrassed by the commotion she caused as well as letting herself freak out like that. "Damn it!" she exclaimed angrily. She walked away, running her hands through her hair.

Jake followed her as they walked away from the crowds who began to mingle and party again. He wondered where she was going and if she would ever slow down long enough for him to catch up.

Finally, she stopped and looked at him. Chloe seemed calmer when she spoke. "Just when you think you have things under control, something happens and you lose it all over again."

Jake didn't say anything. There was no way he could understand the fear she had over almost being raped.

Chloe sighed. "I'm trying so hard."

"I know you are." He could feel her frustration.

She looked at him. "Do you think it will ever go away? All of this shit going on in here?" She pointed to the side of her head.

Jake looked down and then back up at her again. His mind was messed up too. It housed memories of being beaten up and neglected by his mom and dad. Memories of seeing his dead father's broken and bloody body that stunk of alcohol and gasoline. Memories of growing up in a broken home with a drug addict mother who whored around and hated the sight of her only son. "I don't know if it will ever go away, Chloe. Maybe we just learn to deal with it better."

She looked sad. He hated to see her like that. They were doing so good. Turning a new leaf. Somehow, the past always had to surface. He reached out and gently stroked her cheek.

Chloe was looking at him again, her eyes softening. Making his adrenaline pump. He always had her in his heart. But now, he wanted so much more. He wanted to cross that line. He needed to feel her, touch her, kiss her. She was all he had and she was all he wanted. He could tell she felt it too.

"Chloe!" someone was shouting. "There you are!"

Once again, Jake pulled his hand away as Samantha, Jenny and Brooke ran up. They were oblivious to what they had just interrupted.

"Hi, Jake!" they exclaimed. Before he could acknowledge them, they were grabbing Chloe's hand and pulling her away. "You've got to see this!" Brooke said. And just like that, Chloe was being led away by the girls. She awkwardly turned and looked at him, smiling, silently telling him with her eyes that she was sorry.

Jake shook his head disbelievingly as they disappeared. Maybe this was a sign that he and Chloe weren't meant to go further. He wanted her so badly. He felt so sad and disappointed. Perhaps things would be better if they just remained friends. Any hope he had of ever holding her was rapidly fading. What a fool he was for hoping anyway.

Chapter 55

He looked so good lying there, his eyes closed, his bare chest rising up and down with his steady breathing. His handsome face half hidden in the shadows of the room. She stood there watching him sleep. He looked so peaceful. Chloe swore she could stand there forever in the darkness of his room and just watch him. He brought her calmness and serenity. God she loved him. She loved what they had, their friendship, their bond. It was sacred.

But she knew it was time. She couldn't evade this anymore. It was overtaking her, dominating her thoughts, making her pulse race. Even though she loved what they had, it wasn't enough anymore. She wanted to dive deeper. She wanted all of him. She wanted to experience that part of him that through the years had driven all the girls crazy.

Jake stirred in his sleep. He shifted to his side, facing the window, never waking up. Never knowing that she was watching him, her eyes burning. Chloe bit her lower lip. Her heart raced as she slowly crawled onto his bed. She gently settled her body down next to his. Even now, she was still second guessing herself. Was this wrong? It felt so right. She closed her eyes and wrapped her arm around his waist, feeling his stomach muscles across her fingertips as she pulled herself close to him, pressing her cheek against his bare back. She breathed in his scent, feeling the butterflies in her stomach going crazy.

He woke up, turning over quickly to face her. "Chloe? What's wrong? Are you ok?" He was wide awake, a look of fear and concern on his face.

She reached out and touched his cheek. "I'm ok," she whispered lightly. His face softened. She felt his body relaxing. "I just didn't want to be alone tonight."

Jake looked at her, searching her eyes, slowly realizing why she was here in his bed. He didn't say anything. He just reached out and stroked her cheek.

Chloe thought her heart would burst as fast as it was beating. At last, they were here, standing on the edge, ready to fall over at any second. And Chloe was terrified. "What's happening between us….it scares me," she whispered to him.

"It scares me too," he admitted. "I've never been so scared."

She knew he had all the same fears, all the same uncertainties. She put her hand on top of his, closing her eyes, relishing the gentleness of his touch.

She heard his voice in the darkness. "We can take this real slow…"

She opened her eyes again to see his eyes glazed over, looking at her with passion she had never seen. "Ok," she whispered back.

He moved his hand from her face and took hers, intertwining his fingers with hers. They touched foreheads, listening to each other breathe.

"I love you, Chloe." Jake's voice shook. "I've loved you forever."

Chloe squeezed his hand. "I love you too, Jake. You're all I have in this world."

He kissed her gently on the forehead and pulled her closer to him, wrapping his arm around her. At that moment, the whole world could have exploded and it wouldn't have mattered. She was safe. No one and nothing could hurt her now. Chloe fell asleep listening to Jake's heart thudding in his chest.

Chapter 56

How long had he been asleep? He didn't know. But he was awake now. And she was here, lying right next to him. It was Jake's turn to watch her sleep. Her long lashes fluttered on her cheeks as she dreamed. Her silky hair flowed over her bare shoulders. Arousal overtook him as he saw that she was wearing nothing more than a lace bra and matching panties. Her body was amazing, more beautiful than he had ever imagined. His eyes followed the outline of her curves that led from her full breasts to her shapely hips down to her long, lean legs. Her perfect skin glowed in the moonlight.

Jake's hand shook as he reached out, letting his fingers graze her arm, her waist, her hip. Bolts of electricity shot up his arm and through his body. His breathing quickened. She wasn't in the back of his mind anymore. She was right here, underneath his touch. Her eyes were opening now. He was frightened. Would his touch scare her, bring those fears back into her mind that he had witnessed? He wanted her to be ok. To want this too.

She didn't stop him. She reached up and touched his face, letting him know to keep going. Jake couldn't stand it anymore. He had to taste her. Slowly he leaned down, rubbing his face next to hers, grazing her eyes, nose, cheeks with his lips. Lastly, he grazed her lips, barely touching them, driving them both crazy as they both stood on that line they were just about to cross. Jake closed his eyes, ready to dive head first. There was no turning back now. He planted his lips gently upon hers. Their softness overtook him. He pressed harder, forcing her mouth open with his tongue, tasting her sweetness. She pulled him closer, making him kiss her more passionately. For so long, he had fantasized about this, about how it would be. Chloe was taking him to a place he had never been, a place he could never find with anyone else. She rubbed his hair, his neck, his back, turning every part of his body on. She let his hands explore her, discovering parts of her body where no one else was allowed to venture. It was so erotic to hear her moan softly with pleasure, to see her eyes full of lust and passion, knowing he was doing that to her.

Jake laid himself on top of her, pushing himself again her, letting her feel the full extent of his arousal. She gasped softly, holding him close. To his surprise, she allowed him to nestle in between her thighs, brushing his side as she lifted her leg. He moved slowly, rubbing himself against her, wishing he could rip her panties aside and come inside. The heat that radiated from between her legs traveled right through him. He had never wanted anyone more.

Chloe held onto him, moving with him in the dark. He held her arms high above her head, feeling every part of her body as they simulated making love to each other. He kissed her hard on the lips, face and tops of her breasts. Jake listened to her breathing quicken, her soft moans grow louder. He knew what was about to happen. Moving quicker, pushing himself harder against her, he felt her body tense. She arched her neck and back up, her body rising up off the bed. She closed her eyes, her beautiful face reflecting pleasure so powerful it almost looked pained. She erotically screamed, her body twisting underneath him, allowing him to feel all of her muscles tense up. He held onto her, letting her ride the waves of pleasure that overtook her.

When it was over, she was breathing hard, looking at him in the dark. He knew she had never experienced anything like that before. He was awakening something inside of her, reaching deep down where no one had ever been before. He kissed her gently on the lips and then laid his head on her chest, listening to her heart racing. Jake closed his eyes, letting her arms encircle him. Nothing else mattered but being right here. He was so in love with Chloe. She was his everything. And if he had to, he would wait forever for her.

Chapter 57

They pulled up amidst the seemingly hundreds of cars that parked in every nook and cranny of the street. Another rich kid whose parents were out of town was throwing a party. Idling, they stared at the three story modern looking house with glass walls. Inside, they could see people dancing, partying, and hooking up.

Jake shut the pickup off. "They're all going to be shocked."

"I know," Chloe responded, not taking her eyes off the beautiful house. They both got out; Chloe walked around to where Jake was.

He held out his hand. "You ready to do this?"

She grinned and put her hand in his. "Absolutely."

He grinned at her and led the way as they walked up the long walkway towards the front door.

As predicted, once inside, they were bombarded with stares of shock and disbelief. This was Jake and Chloe, best friends since grade school. Sure they were inseparable but no one ever expected to see them actually *together*. Chloe endured dirty looks from girls who weren't afraid to express their disapproval of what they were seeing. Chloe whispered into Jake's ear as they made their way through the crowds, "I've got every girl in here pissed off at me."

Jake squeezed her hand. "Not as pissed off as all the guys are at me. I'm liable to get my ass kicked tonight."

Chloe laughed, squeezing Jake's hand as well. They found Brad and Jeff up ahead, hanging with a bunch of other people. Like everyone else, Brad and Jeff watched with surprise at seeing their two best friends holding hands.

"Hi, fellas," responded Chloe, smiling at her buddies.

Brad and Jeff glanced down at their intertwined fingers. Jake knew it was just so strange for them to see him and Chloe like this. They quickly looked back up at Chloe and grinned. "Hey, Chloe. You're looking good tonight," responded Brad. Jeff nodded in agreement.

Chloe smiled shyly. Someone began calling her name from across the room. Samantha waved for her to come over. Chloe turned to Jake. "I'll be back." She reluctantly let go of his hand and sauntered off, leaving Jake, Brad & Jeff staring after her.

Brad turned to Jake, grinning. "So you and Chloe, huh?" He patted his friend on the shoulder.

Jake blushed, smiling from ear to ear. "Yeah," he responded, trying to play down his happiness.

Jeff leaned in. "So how is it?"

Jake couldn't stop smiling. "It's good. Real good," he replied calmly. What he really wanted to do was to jump up and down like a madman and tell everyone around him how incredible it was to be so in love with Chloe Mayer. But he decided it was probably better to remain cool. He pointed a finger at his buddies. "So you guys can't be looking at her like that anymore."

Jeff laughed, looking over at Chloe. "I think *us* looking at her like that is the least of your problems." He nodded his head in her direction.

Jake turned to see a group of guys surrounding her as she tried to talk to Samantha and the other girls. They obviously didn't see him and Chloe walking in hand in hand or else they just didn't care. But seeing all those guys staring at Chloe with adoration didn't make Jake upset or jealous. It made him proud. Proud because he knew that no matter what happened, she was his. All his.

Chapter 58

The guys that surrounded Chloe and her girlfriends were relentless. Sure they were good looking but funny how when you were in love with someone, you only had eyes for that person. Chloe stole a glance at her man. *Her man*. God that sounded so corny but she liked it. He was grinning at her too, making her heart skip a beat.

Samantha nudged her. "So you and Jake, huh?" She was smiling.

It was Chloe's turn to blush. "Yeah," was all she managed to say.

"It's about time! I am so happy for you!" Her eyes were sparkling at Chloe.

Chloe looked down and then back up. "Thanks. I'm happy too."

"I can tell. You're absolutely beaming!" She jokingly nudged Chloe again. And then Samantha looked over at Jake and frowned. "Uh-oh, trouble."

Chloe glanced over to see a group of girls surrounding Jake and the guys. They looked to be on the prowl, flirting with their bodies, standing as close as they could.

Samantha rolled her eyes. "Doesn't that make you mad?"

Before Chloe could answer, some guy was in *her* face, trying to make small talk. *Speaking of being on the prowl…*Chloe had to giggle at the guy. None the less, she remained friendly. Before she knew it, she, Samantha and the other girls were wrapped up in flirtatious advances and comments of their own. In the midst of it all, Chloe stole a glance over at Jake and the guys. They seemed to be having the same problem. Chloe watched as a pretty red head touched Jake on the arm, flirting effortlessly. Before anyone knew what was happening, the red head lifted up her top and flashed Jake her bare breasts. Holy shit! She was so drunk. Jake's eyes grew wide with shock. Brad and Jeff nearly jumped over his shoulders to catch a closer glimpse. Chloe laughed. She laughed out loud that the guy she was talking to looked at her like she was crazy.

Jake looked over at her, not sure what to do next. He laughed too when he saw Chloe's reaction. Chloe shook her head incredulously at him and turned her attention back to the guy who was trying so hard to impress her. He had no idea that Chloe wanted nothing more than to be by Jake's side. She decided to let this guy off easy. Chloe excused herself.

But before she could walk away, Samantha was grabbing her arm. "You're not leaving me alone with these sharks! Come on…let's go over here for a minute."

Chloe motioned towards the opposite direction. "But Jake…."

Samantha rolled her eyes again. "You have all night to be with Jake. There's a guy over here I'm interested in. Tell me what you think." She was dragging Chloe off, further away from Jake. Chloe looked over her shoulder at him, wishing she could be with him. Instead, she sighed and followed Samantha into another part of the glorious glass house they were in.

Chapter 59

Jake sighed. Big breasts were staring him in the face. This girl was wasted. "Ok, I think I've seen enough," he told her.

She pouted, pulling her shirt back down. "You don't like them? My mom gave them to me as a graduation present."

"Well, that's nice…and *they're* very nice. It's just that…I've got a girlfriend." Man, that felt so good to say. He had never said that before.

The redhead put her hands on her hips. She wasn't used to being turned down. "Oh yeah? I don't believe you. Where is she?"

"She's right over….there." Jake pointed to the other side of the room only to see Chloe being drug off further away. Damn, where was she going now?

"Looks like she's doing her own thing tonight," replied the redhead coyly. "Don't worry, I'll keep you company." She inched closer, her intentions out in the open.

Brad and Jeff gave Jake a knowing look. Normally, presented with an opportunity like this, they would see their friend disappearing with this girl. But Jake played it cool. He stepped back. "I'm going to catch up with her." He smiled at the disappointed red head and began to walk towards the direction he had last seen Chloe.

Jake hadn't taken two steps when someone was dragging him by the arm. "Jake! I've got some people over here who want to meet you!" This time it was Jake's turn to be shuffled off amongst the crowds. Before he knew it…he was somewhere on the third floor. Jake wondered if he'd ever meet up with Chloe. If he caught a glimpse of her, she'd be across the room, on another floor, or outside lost in a sea of people. Her sexy new look made her quite popular. Everyone wanted to be with her. But he could tell, even through all the chaos that surrounded them, it was *him* that she wanted. Her eyes teased him, tempted him, made his pulse race. She was just so beautiful. But no matter how hard they tried, it seemed impossible for them to get back together. They spent most of the night trying to excuse themselves from whomever they were talking to only to get dragged off or intercepted by someone else.

Jake glanced at his watch. It was midnight. His head was buzzing from the nonstop commotion and noise. But he had long tuned out what all the people around him were talking about, because *she* was driving him crazy. He was seeing her across the room with guys all over her, trying to get one shot at her. She was toying with them, flirting harmlessly, leading them on and making them think she was interested. But all the while, she was looking at him, telling him silently that it was him that she wanted. He eyed her amazing body. He was ready to taste her again. God, he said he would be mature about this. Take things slow. Focus on just being with her. But she was like a drug, the perfect high. He had to take another hit. She did that to him. Like no one else before her. She was feeling it too. He could tell, from that very first night. She wanted to let go. Her innocence was the only thing stopping her.

Chloe was smiling at him now. Smiling in that way that meant only one thing. He couldn't hold out anymore. If he had to shove someone off, that's what he would do to get to her. From across the room, she understood his look of determination. She was making her way towards him too.

Chapter 60

"Chloe! Over here, Chloe!" someone was calling.

Chloe shook her head no. "I'll catch up with you later," she hollered back. She was on a mission.

"Hey sweetie, wanna dance?" another guy was asking.

"Maybe later," she responded, not seeing his face. The only face she was focusing on was Jake's. She had held out as long as she could and had been patient all night. But now, she had to give in to that craving. That craving that only he could satisfy. It was like a euphoria she couldn't describe. He looked so good, walking towards her like that, his eyes burning a hole right through her.

At last, they were face to face, everyone around them disappearing. He rubbed her arms, making shivers run up and down her spine. "Hi," he grinned.

"Hi," she grinned back.

"Wanna get out of here?" he asked, making her heart speed up.

"I thought you'd never ask," she breathlessly replied. He took her hand and they quickly made their way through the crowds. Just being with him made Chloe lightheaded. She could hardly catch her breath. The anticipation was driving her crazy.

They were outside, away from the chaos and loud music. Chloe couldn't hold out any longer. She pounced on him, kissing him right there in the middle of the drive, taking his breath away. "I've missed you, Jake! I can't stand not being with you!" She was ready to let go with him again.

He grinned at her and then he took her hand. "Come on!" They hurried to his pickup and hopped in. Once inside, Jake pulled her close, kissing her passionately. She loved how she felt when she was with him. The exhilaration running through her body was indescribable. He reluctantly pulled away, playfully groaning in frustration. "Arrrggghhh! You're making me nuts!"

Chloe threw her head back and laughed as Jake started up the vehicle. She scooted next to him, feeling so secure when he wrapped his arm around her shoulders. She laid her head against him, listening to the sound of the roaring engine as they drove towards their secret hiding place.

Jake parked the pickup in the clearing. He turned and looked at her. Even in the shadows of the cab, Chloe could see his eyes shining at her. He reached out and touched her cheek, making her stomach flutter. It still amazed her that they were here…in this place that they had been so scared to find for so long. She loved him so much and she knew that the bond they had always shared was deepening now. It was growing stronger with this new found fascination that they had for each other.

He had told her they could take things slow. But Chloe couldn't stop what she was feeling. Jake did something to her. She wanted to be so close to him and discover sides of him she had never let herself know…until now. "No one will ever know how much I truly love you," she told him, her voice shaking with excitement.

Jake pulled her close, wrapping his arms around her. "*I know,*" he whispered tenderly. "And that's all that matters." He kissed her softly. She fell with him into a world of elation and desire. For the rest of the night, they became lost in each other with no fear or inhibition, and absolutely no intentions of ever being found.

Chapter 61

It was inevitable. The phone call from Cambridge made her realize it even more, delivering news that was bittersweet. She had a great job lined up, working right there on campus with the law professors. Now she had no worries about cash flow. But they wanted her there the Monday after graduation. She would be a gopher for their summer research projects. It was a golden opportunity to jump-start her studies. But that meant leaving Jake sooner than she had anticipated. How would he take the news?

Chloe sat down at her kitchen table and sighed. It was in the back of both of their minds and neither of them wanted to bring it up. She felt like an ostrich sticking its head in the sand to avoid the obvious. Chloe just knew if they talked about it, she would lose it. And they had been so happy. For once in their lives, they had put everything else on hold and had just enjoyed being with each other, living every moment they had with each other to the fullest. But the inevitable was still there, eating at them.

Chloe looked around her kitchen. Graduation was less than a month away. The house was hers. She just couldn't up and leave. It wasn't that simple. Nothing ever was. Her dad was gone, out of her life forever. It was all up to her now. At 18, Chloe had experienced more than most people in their 20's. It had hardened her, but at the same time, she had the strength and maturity to deal with things that most people her age had no clue about. Figuring out what to do with the house was just another stepping stone for her towards her new life. Chloe picked up the phone book and looked under the yellow pages under realtors. She had to sell the house and fast. And all the stuff in it? She flipped the pages until she found the heading "storage units". Perhaps she'd come back for it one day. But for now, it would get left behind, just like everything else in her old life.

Chapter 62

Brad Wilson & Jeff Allen were best friends and had been since sixth grade when they met on the playground. They had a lot in common. Both came from broken homes with absent fathers. Brad's parents divorced when he was 2. He never knew his dad. Jeff's parents divorced when he was 3. He barely remembered his dad. And their single parent mothers? Well, maybe it had been too hard raising a son on their own. Whatever the reasons were, they were absent in their sons' lives. Perhaps that's why Brad and Jeff immediately connected with Jake and Chloe.

The four were products of parents who just didn't care. They came to rely on each other for their needs, never judging each other, and always being there to offer a shoulder. Through the years, it never changed. It only grew stronger. But soon, all of it was going to end. They were all going to go their separate ways in order to find out who they would become.

These impending changes weighed heavily on their minds. Especially now as Brad, Jeff and Jake sat around a small fire at "The Diamond Hills", all of them in melancholy moods. No party was raging tonight. Only open space, surrounded by tall pine trees and a billion stars up above. The only thing dancing were the flames that crackled the wood. The three friends stared into the mesmerizing glow.

"I can't believe in several weeks, it's all going to be over. No more high school," replied Jeff.

"And then the real world begins" added Brad.

Jake snickered. "I think the real world began for all of us when our dads dropped out of our lives," reflecting on all that they had to go through growing up in broken homes.

Jeff and Brad nodded. "You're right," replied Brad softly.

Jeff, the ever crazy, wild one of the bunch laughed. "But it's been one hell of a ride!" He always got a rise out of his friends. They both laughed along with him.

"So Chloe should have told her boss to piss off. He's a slave driver, making her work like this on a school night," said Brad.

Jake shrugged. "She needs the money." He paused for a minute and then looked at his buddies. "Her house went on the market today."

If he didn't want them to notice, it didn't work. They knew him too well. Brad and Jeff detected the sadness in his voice right away. "Maybe you could transfer after a year or two," offered Jeff.

Jake shook his head and looked down. "I don't even know if I'm going at all."

Brad piped up. "Dude, you've got a free ride. You have to go."

"And do what with my mother? She's a wreck."

"You can't put your life on hold forever," explained Jeff.

Jake ignored him. "She'll lose the house. She'll wind up on the streets for good."

Brad shook his head in disappointment. "You're 18 years old. You shouldn't have to deal with this shit, especially when you have the opportunity to get out of this hell hole."

Jake looked down. "Yeah, well, I've been dealing with this shit all my life."

Brad and Jeff said nothing. It just sucked. They should all be happy. But instead, it seemed more hard knocks were coming.

"And Chloe's dad? Does anybody know where that bastard is?" asked Brad.

Jake shook his head no.

Jeff frowned. "I always hated that asshole. That coward just abandoned her."

Jake looked down again. Talking about Chloe made his sadness more evident. Over the past couple of months, Brad and Jeff watched as Jake and Chloe fell madly in love with each other. Jake was never happier than when he was with her. His eyes shone. He laughed. He was so alive. No other girl ever had that effect on their friend and they had seen plenty try to steal Jake's heart through the years. So really, it was no surprise when Jake and Chloe finally hooked up. Brad and Jeff had seen it from the beginning. Jake had always loved her. He was just too scared to admit it.

And now, so much uncertainty surrounded them. Brad and Jeff picked up on that. They hated to see their good friends tormented by the future. Jake and Chloe had always had each other since they were little kids. What was going to happen now?

Jake looked up towards his two friends. "You guys are like brothers to me. We've been through a lot of shit together."

Brad and Jeff nodded in agreement.

Jake continued. "So promise me, no matter what happens or how far we drift apart, that one day…when it counts, we'll all find each other again."

Brad and Jeff didn't say anything. They didn't have to. They all extended their fists towards each other, touching knuckles. And it was just understood.

Chapter 63

Jake was tired when he walked through his front door into his empty house. Work had been hard, but Jake was one of their best workers. He was strong, diligent and always gave a hundred percent. He outworked most of the other guys out there, reflecting self-discipline and commitment.

Evening was falling now. And Jake still had homework to do. He sat down at the kitchen table, wishing Chloe was here. She always made him feel better. Just then the phone rang. Jake smiled. That was probably her calling to tell him she would stop by as soon as she got off work herself. He answered cheerfully.

"Jake Stevens?" came the rigid female voice on the other end.

"Yes?"

"This is Nurse Randalls. I'm calling from Wilson General Hospital." There was a pause and Jake's heart started to race. "Your mother's been in an accident. You better get down here."

Five minutes later, Jake skidded into the hospital parking lot. He ran through the emergency room doors, frantically asking where his mother was. A nurse led him down a long hallway and through some doors labeled "ICU". Jake walked into a room where his mother lay, hooked up to a million tubes and monitors. She was unrecognizable. Her face was bruised and scabbed; her body, broken. Jake stared at her, unable to speak. The nurse told him she would get the doctor.

A few minutes later, a man in a white coat walked in. "Jake Stevens?"

Jake turned and looked at him. The man extended his hand. Jake couldn't move to shake it. The doctor seemed to understand. He pulled his hand back.

"I'm Dr. Underwood. Your mother was hit by a car. She sustained some serious internal injuries, broken bones, a collapsed lung and severe head trauma. We had to perform emergency surgery to stop the bleeding. It's under control for now." He spoke in a monotone. And then Dr. Underwood sighed. "But her drug use is making the healing process very difficult."

Jake locked eyes with Dr. Underwood but said nothing. He didn't know what to say. He was in too much shock. And so he just looked back at her, his mother.

Dr. Underwood continued. "When was the last time you saw your mother?"

"Several weeks ago," Jake managed to stammer out.

"According to the police report and eyewitnesses, she was running away from a drug dealer. She had no I.D. on her." The doctor pulled something out of his pocket and handed it to Jake. "Just a picture of you."

Jake looked at the weathered, wrinkled photo. It was his 1st grade school picture. Staring back at him was a scared looking little boy who had a forced smile on his face displaying two missing front teeth. *Jesus Christ.*

"Miraculously, someone recognized that it was you."

Jake shook his head and handed the picture back to the doctor. "What are her chances?"

Dr. Underwood looked down and then back up again. "Not very good. It's hard to say what the outcome will be. She may be brain damaged. She may slip into a coma. It's too soon to tell."

Jake looked at the woman who gave him life. It was the only thing that she gave him. So why did he feel so devastated? Why did he even care? She never loved him. He had always been the burden, the bad reminder of the shitty life she hated so much. Yet his heart wrenched as he looked at her lifeless body. Jake felt the doctor's hand on his shoulder.

"I'm sorry, son," he heard the doctor tell him. And then the doctor left.

Chapter 64

Chloe was relieved when she saw Jake's pickup parked amongst the trees in their secret hiding place. She got out of her car and walked up to him. He was sitting behind the steering wheel, staring out at nothing. She opened the passenger side door and crawled in. He slowly turned to her, his eyes red and puffy from crying. She reached out and touched his shoulder. "The nurses said you left a while ago. I figured you'd be here."

He didn't say anything. Jake just started tearing up again.

Chloe's heart ached for him. She could feel the pain he was feeling. "I'm so sorry, Jake."

He looked up at her. "I had to leave, Chloe. I had to get out of there. Because the only thing I could think about was how much better it would all be if she would just die…!" He sobbed. "I'm so selfish. I'm so horrible. What kind of son wishes his mother would just die!" He sobbed, mumbling over and over again what a terrible person he was.

Chloe pulled him into her arms and just let him cry like a little baby. She cried too, not knowing what to do or say. She saw his mother. It was just awful. To Chloe, Clarissa Stevens looked like she was already dead.

Jake calmed down slightly, sniffling. "What am I gonna do? We've got finals coming up. How am I going to graduate?"

"We'll work this out, Jake. We'll talk to Mr. Jackson tomorrow at school. He'll make an exception."

"I can't believe this is happening. What am I gonna do? What am I gonna do?" he repeated, crying all over again.

Chloe tried her best to calm him. "Shhh, Jake. It's going to be alright. We'll get through this together. I promise." She held him tightly until he quit crying. "Come on, Jake. Let's get back to the hospital."

Chapter 65

    Clarissa Stevens did not have health insurance. She didn't even have a life insurance policy. She had nothing. Not only did Jake have his grief and guilt to weigh him down, he was facing the realization of how he would soon be bombarded by hospital bills. How the hell was he going to pay them when he struggled to pay his regular bills?

    School was rapidly coming to an end. Yet here Jake was, running back and forth between work and the hospital, missing what should have been the best time of his life. While other seniors at school studied for finals, attended prom and other year end senior activities, Jake busted his ass at his construction job, putting in overtime when he could to earn extra money and then sitting by his mother's side filling out mounds of hospital paperwork, talking to doctors and nurses about his mother's grim diagnosis. When he could, he would squeeze in his studies at school or take assignments to work on at home. Jake wasn't going to graduate with his class. Mr. Jackson already informed of that fact. He would have to make up what he was missing in some summer classes. It all seemed hopeless. Thank God for Brad, Jeff and of course Chloe. They visited almost everyday, lending any kind of support they could. He realized just how lucky he was to have such good friends.

Jake's mother never woke up. The doctors said she was in a coma now. They couldn't offer any news on how long they expected her to stay like that. It could be days, weeks, months, maybe even years. Jake took the news hard. What the hell was he supposed to do now? He had so many questions, so many thoughts running through his head. It overwhelmed him. He was physically and mentally exhausted. He felt like he had just been handed a life sentence in prison. The bars were slamming shut all around him. He just wanted to crouch in the corner of his cell and shut himself off.

Someone was kissing him gently on the cheek. Jake opened his tired eyes and saw Chloe smiling down at him. He sat upright in his chair and closed his open calculus book. "Hey," he replied as he set his book on the night stand beside his mother's bed.

"Hi," she responded. "I heard," she said as she nodded towards Clarissa. "They have no idea how long she could be like that?"

He shook his head no.

She walked over to the bed, staring down at Clarissa. "I'm not going, Jake," she replied softly.

Jake frowned. "What?"

She turned and faced him. "To Harvard. I'm not going. I can't leave you like this."

Jake stood up. "What are you talking about? You have to go."

"No I don't. I need to be with you. I need to help you through this."

"Chloe, don't be ridiculous! You have a full ride scholarship. You have a great job lined up. You can't just pass all that up."

"Yes I can! I need to stay and help you take care of her. I can't abandon you like this!"

Jake walked up to her and put his hands on her shoulders. "Chloe, we promised each other. We said we would do whatever it took to make it out of all this. We said we would go our separate ways when it was time, to find ourselves without each other."

Chloe's eyes became watery. "I didn't expect all of this to happen." She waved her hand over Clarissa's bed. "I didn't expect to see your whole world come crumbling down." She paused, trying to catch her breath. "I didn't expect to fall so in love with you."

Jake's eyes watered too. "You can't do this. You can't stay."

She became angry. "Why not? Don't you love me too?"

"How can you even ask me that?" It was his turn to get angry.

"I don't understand! I want to help you! I want to be here for you!" She wiped the tears that were falling freely now.

Jake was so tired. He was so emotionally distraught. "Chloe! Stop it! Shut up! Just shut up, ok! This is crazy. You're not staying! Period! Quit being stupid!"

She froze, his harsh words slapping her in the face. Jake regretted them as soon as they spilled out of his mouth. But it was too late. She glared at him. "I never thought I would see this day."

He ran his fingers through his hair. "What are you talking about?!" he shouted, unable to contain his anger now, even though he knew it was hurting her.

"The day when you pushed me away!" she hollered back. Fresh tears stung her eyes as she turned and ran out.

Jake wanted to run after her. He wanted to grab her and hold her in his arms forever and tell her he was so sorry for being the biggest jerk. He wanted to tell her over and over again how much he loved her and that she would never know how much she truly meant to him.

But he didn't. He just slumped down into his chair and buried his face into his hands.

Chapter 66

No matter how many times her dad had hit her, verbally abused her or emotionally neglected her, it didn't hurt as much as she was hurting now. No matter how awful it was to be a scared little girl who had a mother who cried all the time, who laid curled up in bed all day, who stared at her with blank eyes and who eventually slit her wrists and abandoned her, it didn't hurt as much as she was hurting now. None of it hurt nearly as badly as losing Jake. He was gone. Emotionally, physically, Jake was gone. She could see it in his eyes. The little boy who took her under his wing so long ago, sheltered her from all the bad things and made her smile didn't need her anymore. The young man who stole her heart, touched her so emotionally and made her feel so beautiful had pushed her away.

Jake was her best friend whom she loved more than anything. But years of abuse and neglect had hardened her. Even though she was absolutely devastated, continuing to cry over it was just not an option. She became numb to it, closing herself off to the emotions; something she learned to do a long time ago in order to cope.

Someone was knocking on her front door, startling her out of her thoughts. Chloe looked at her alarm clock and realized the movers were here. Today was the day all of her stuff was going into storage.

Her house had sold. In two days time, Chloe would graduate high school and leave this world behind. Including Jake.

Yes, he had been right. She had told him the day would come when they would have to do this, find their own way. They had always had each other. The time would come when they would have to discover the person they were meant to become without the other. Chloe sighed. She just never thought it would be like this. It was not how she ever imagined. It was hurting like hell.

The knocking continued, reminding her that the world wasn't stopping for anyone. Chloe gathered herself up and headed downstairs. Once the movers began moving boxes and furniture, Chloe came to the realization that there was absolutely no turning back now.

Chapter 67

Evening was quickly falling. Jeff knocked on Chloe's front door, hoping she would answer. The door swung open, leaving Jeff staring Chloe in the face. He didn't think he had ever seen her so sad or so lost, not even after her father had beaten her up or when Ty nearly raped her. The glow she had exuded the last several months was gone. "Can I come in?" he asked.

Chloe stepped aside. He walked in, staring at the empty room. All the furniture was gone. Only a few boxes remained.

"I can't believe it's really happening," he replied, looking around.

Chloe looked around too. "I'm leaving first thing Sunday morning."

Jeff had always been the wild one. The guy who always got the fun started, who made everyone laugh, who always raised hell. But tonight, he didn't feel like cracking any jokes. He just wanted to save his two best friends. "I just came from the hospital."

Chloe looked away and walked towards the window, staring out into the street.

Jeff walked up behind her. "Chloe, please. Don't end things this way. It's killing him."

Chloe faced Jeff. "He made it perfectly clear. He doesn't want me to stay."

Jeff ran his fingers through his blonde hair. "You're the only girl he's ever loved, Chloe. Hell, for that matter, you're probably the only girl he'll ever love as screwed up as he is." Jeff hesitated. "Don't you see?"

Chloe searched Jeff's face.

Jeff continued. "If you stayed, if you gave up the one opportunity to get out of this dark and twisted world you all have lived in for so long, if you didn't take the chance to turn your life into something positive and make something of yourself, he would never forgive himself for that. For being the cause of keeping you from becoming what he's always known you should be."

Chloe felt the tears welling up in her eyes. "But what about him? What about his chance? His one opportunity? It got ripped away from him! I just can't leave him like that. Someone needs to be there for him. To help him!"

Jeff put his hand on Chloe's shoulder. "None of us can help him, Chloe. This is something he's going to have to figure out for himself. And I think he realizes that too."

Chloe wiped the tears from her eyes. "I just love him."

Jeff smiled, hugging Chloe. "Then tell him, Chloe. Show him. Please…" he pleaded with her, "don't leave without saying goodbye."

Chapter 68

Jeff, Brad and Chloe stood in the middle of the football field amongst hundreds of other graduates. They stared at each other, realizing this was probably one of the last times they would be together. Brad sighed, holding onto his diploma. "It's just not the same with one of us missing."

Jeff looked at Chloe in her cap and gown. And then at Brad in his. "He'll be alright. He's going to get through this."

Chloe looked down. She was so sad. She had not gone to see Jake since the night she ran out on him. It was hard to hear her friends talk about him. She tried to smile, tried to be happy in the moment that they were in. But they saw right through her. "I'm going to miss you guys." She was so proud of them. They both looked so handsome standing there.

"Do you think we'll stay in touch?" asked Brad.

"I'd like to think so," she replied softly. But Chloe was a realist. People changed and drifted apart all the time.

Jeff smiled. "Enough of this mushy talk. It's time to party! No more high school!"

Brad laughed at his crazy friend. "That's right. It's time to celebrate. Chloe, you are coming tonight, aren't you?"

Chloe looked down again. "I don't know. I've got to get up pretty early tomorrow."

Jeff threw his arm around her shoulder. "Chloe…it's going to be the biggest bash at "The Hills" yet. It's our graduation party! The last party at "The Diamond Hills". Our last chance to act totally insane before we have to become responsible adults."

Brad threw his arm around Chloe as well. "That's right. You have to come." They ribbed her and teased her until they had her laughing.

"Ok, ok. I'll be there." She hugged them both, kissing them on the cheek. "I love you guys. I don't know what I would have done without you."

Chapter 69

The nurses told him to go out and have some fun with his friends. It was graduation night. They would keep an eye on his mother. "Go be a kid for one night," they told him. Jake had been in another world since his mother's accident. School, friends, parties…they all seemed a part of another life that he used to know. He felt like he had been a million miles away.

But God, did he miss Chloe. His heart ached for her. He just wanted to see her. To tell her he was sorry. To touch her one last time before she was gone for good. He couldn't believe it was actually happening. He had always known this day would come but he never thought it would be this devastating, this hard to handle. She was right. He never thought they would fall so deeply in love with each other either, making their promises that much harder to keep. And he did love her. People always say that at 18, you can't possibly know what true love is. Well if this wasn't true love, Jake didn't know what else it could be.

And so for the sake of running into her, he decided to go. Would she even talk to him? Did she hate him? It would kill him if he couldn't tell her goodbye.

Jake went home and showered. He looked at himself in the mirror as he shaved. He was unrecognizable. He had dark circles under his eyes. He was a little leaner from not eating well. But his muscles seemed more defined from working so hard at his construction job. He was sore and tired, both physically and mentally. He didn't feel 18. He felt like the weight of the world on his shoulders had turned him into a man.

It was almost 11 pm by the time Jake showed up at "The Diamond Hills". The graduation party was in full swing. Most everyone was well on their way to being intoxicated if they weren't already there. Jake almost felt out of place. He didn't have a reason to celebrate like everyone else around him did. But as people came up to him, asking about his mother and wishing him all the best, Jake could feel himself relaxing a bit. His peers asked about summer school and when he would receive his diploma. He was polite, patiently explaining his situation to anyone who asked, the whole time looking for Chloe. He couldn't find her. Just as his heart was about to sink, he spotted Brad and Jeff. His buddies always knew how to make him smile. He walked up to them. They hugged him, telling him how glad they were that he showed up. "Congratulations, guys! How does it feel?" he asked.

"It's good, Jake," replied Brad.

"I'm sorry I couldn't make it this morning," Jake responded, referring to the graduation ceremony.

Jeff playfully slapped him on the back. "We understand. You don't have to apologize."

Brad agreed. "That's right. And hey, in a month and half, you'll be there too."

Jake shook his head. "Yeah, I'm ready to get this over with." He glanced around the scene. People were starting to get crazy. "It's one hell of a party."

Jeff smiled, looking at some girls who were eyeing him. "Yep, one last romp before adulthood begins."

Jake laughed. And then he grew serious. "Have you seen Chloe anywhere?"

Brad and Jeff sensed his urgency. Brad nodded up towards the hill. "She's right over there with the girls. I was afraid she wouldn't show either. It took some convincing."

Jake looked up at her. She was surrounded by her girlfriends. All of them were laughing and having a good time. All of them except for Chloe. She just stood amongst them, looking lost, just like she always used to. He could tell she was hurting too. Seeing her made Jake so sad. Just several weeks ago, they had had everything. The world was theirs. And they sat on top of it, so in love with each other. God, he wished he could get that back. He'd give anything to go back to that place.

Chloe finally caught sight of him. She literally froze. He couldn't read her. She seemed numb, her eyes not telling him anything. And then all of a sudden, she was bidding her friends goodbye, hugging them, wishing them all well.

Jake watched broken hearted as she slowly walked away from the party and drove away. "She hates me," he replied, his voice shaking.

Brad and Jeff witnessed it too. "She doesn't hate you, Jake. She loves you," Jeff told him. "She told me she did."

Jake turned to his friends, trying to hide his anguish. "How do I fix this?" He was begging them for an answer.

Brad shoved his hands in his pockets. "You go and tell her goodbye."

Jake began tearing up, quickly trying to wipe at his eyes. Damn it! He didn't want them to see him like this. To see how much this was tearing him up inside. "What if she won't talk to me?"

Jeff put his hand on Jake's shoulder. "Jake…have you forgotten? This is our girl, Chloe. The greatest girl in the world." He smiled at Jake, giving him the confidence and support he needed.

Jake's heart pounded as he drove on the winding roads and up the hills that led to their secret hiding place. If she wasn't there, then he would know it just wasn't meant to be. Chloe would be gone forever and that would be it. She would be out of his life for good. And he would be left with the biggest regret that he knew would eat at him for the rest of his days. He closed his eyes for a second and prayed. Prayed that when he topped the hill, he would find her. *Please, God, let her be there.*

Jake opened his eyes and almost cried out loud when he saw her car parked in the clearing. He stopped the pickup, wanting to leap out and run up to her. But how would she take him showing up here? Would she even want to see him? Jake slowly got out and walked up. She was laying on the hood of her car, her back against the windshield, looking up at the stars.

Jake gulped hard. He felt his whole body shaking as he came up beside her. She slowly turned, nothing in her eyes. And then, a smile. The most beautiful smile spread across her pretty face.

"Hi," she softly said.

Relief flooded his body. "Hi," he replied, trying to steady his voice.

"Fitting isn't it?" she commented, a calmness and peace about her.

"What do you mean?" he asked.

"Ending this in the place where it all began." She waved her hand towards the trees.

Jake looked down, not sure what to say, even though a million thoughts were flooding his brain. He looked back up at her. "I'm so sorry, Chloe…"

She sat up and swung her legs over the side of the car. "Shhh. Don't apologize." She held out her hand to him. He graciously took it and hopped onto the car beside her. She intertwined her fingers with his. It felt so good to touch her again. "I understand now, Jake. This is something we've got to do." She looked him in the eyes and squeezed his hand. "So I want to remember being happy with you. Like when we were little kids and nothing else mattered as long as we had each other. Remember that?"

Jake nodded.

Chloe leaned her head on his shoulder and closed her eyes. She was smiling, perhaps remembering a childhood memory. Jake was just sure he was looking at an angel. Her long, dark lashes graced her smooth cheeks. She opened her eyes again. They gleamed with the excitement of a child. "Come on!" she called as she hopped down and dug around in the back of her fully loaded car. Jake watched as she pulled out a blanket and draped it on the ground. She plopped down, leaning back on her hands with her legs outstretched in front of her. She patted the spot right beside her. He smiled as he sat down. She grinned at him. "Just like the first time…minus the cookies."

Jake laughed. "And the flashlight and of course the stories of Bigfoot."

Chloe laughed, throwing her head back. "And I believed every bit of it too!"

Jake laughed harder, recalling that fateful night, the night that sealed his unbreakable bond with Chloe. He would never forget it. Just like he would never forget this moment. This very moment right now and how Chloe was smiling at him and looking at him in that way. It made him feel so good. Just like time was standing still. But he knew the sun would be rising and all of this would come to an end. As much as Chloe was trying to mask it, he could tell she knew it too. They were doing everything they could to keep from falling apart.

She nudged him with her shoulder. He looked at her. She grew serious. "You promise you're going to be ok?" she asked, her voice soft and low.

He studied her face for a second. She always put him first. She always made him feel special. He nodded. "Yeah. I'll be ok…as long as I know you'll be ok."

Chloe looked forward, staring at the swaying trees. She didn't say a word. And then she turned back to him. "I want to give you something, Jake."

He was puzzled, not sure what she was talking about.

She continued. "Something to remember me by. And something that I can take with me too…forever."

Jake studied her again, searching her eyes. And then he knew. His heart began to pound. She was serious as could be. He was at a loss for words.

She leaned in and kissed him tenderly on the lips. "I've always dreamed of this moment. I had always prayed it would be you. Deep in my heart, I was always saving myself for you."

Jake swallowed hard, feeling himself get lightheaded. The months they had been together, they couldn't keep their hands off of each other. But he had never pressured her. He had never asked. He loved her too much. And now, it was going to happen. He had always dreamed of this moment too.

She was kissing him again, more passionately now, arousing him, touching his face with her fingertips. "I want to remember you, over and over again tonight…until the sun comes up," she whispered into his ear.

With a shaking hand, Jake reached for her blouse and began unbuttoning it. He wasn't going to think about tomorrow and what that would bring. Tonight was theirs. For one last time, he was going to hold Chloe and make her never forget what they once had.

Chapter 70

Chloe lay completely naked on the blanket. She watched as Jake's eyes scanned her from head to toe, drinking her all in, burning the image of her body into his mind. He didn't have to speak. She knew that he loved her with all of his heart and soul. He took his shirt off, exposing his amazing body. She felt the butterflies. God it felt so good to feel this way again. He was making her forget. He was making her crazy with lust and desire. She wasn't scared. She wasn't hesitant. She wanted this more than anything in the world.

He laid himself down on top of her, holding her tightly. She wrapped her arms around him too, feeling every part of his body pressing against hers. The stars sparkled above her, making her feel as if they were floating. She was trembling. Trembling from excitement, from anticipation of the unknown.

"Are you ok?" he whispered tenderly.

She nodded yes. He kissed her slow and deep, stirring emotions up inside of her. No fear, no nightmares, no shattered fragments in her mind. They were all gone. Jake made them disappear. She felt him entering her, slow and gently. The heat from his body consumed her as he ever so tenderly penetrated her. She felt the slight pressure and pain of losing her virginity. And God, it felt so right. This was where she belonged. With Jake, giving herself to him completely, their bodies becoming one. She kept her eyes closed and held on to him, knowing that nothing else mattered right now. She felt him filling her up, touching the deepest part of her. He began stroking, back and forth, never letting go of her, kissing her on her eyes, nose, cheeks, and neck. She felt the pain subside. Pleasure like she had never known began taking over. It started from deep inside of her, where he was at, and radiated outward and upward, spreading through her whole body. She opened her legs wider, feeling him go deeper with each stroke. Chloe rubbed her hands along his back, pulling him closer into her. "Oh, God, Jake," she whispered. "It feels so good….you feel so good."

"You do too, Chloe. You have no idea how good you feel," he whispered back. He held her arms up over her head and began pushing harder, faster. She moaned, throwing her head back, arching her body and thrusting her hips up to meet his. They made love as if they were the last two people on earth. No one around but just a billion stars.

And then she felt herself climaxing.

Jake felt it too. "Come with me, Chloe. Hold on tight and come with me," he told her. She wrapped her body around his and let herself go, feeling the explosion from deep inside of her. Every muscle in her body went into erotic spasms. Chloe felt Jake explode inside of her too, his body riding waves of pleasure, until finally, he collapsed on top of her. They laid against each other, breathing heavily, trying to catch their breath. Chloe felt Jake's heart racing in his chest. She felt so close to him, like she could crawl inside of him. No one had ever made her feel this way.

A slight breeze came up, gracing their naked bodies. Jake rolled off of her and laid beside her, staring up at the night sky. She watched his strong chest moving up and down as he breathed. She couldn't believe they had just made love. Had just shared each other's bodies with one another. Had been as close as two people could possibly be. It was better than she had ever imagined. She reached out and touched his stomach. It quivered underneath her touch. He was so handsome. Chloe knew from that moment on, she could never love anyone like she loved Jake.

He turned and looked at her. "What are you thinking?" he asked.

She scanned his chiseled body and grinned. "I'm thinking, 'Now I know what all the girls were talking about!'"

Jake threw his head back and laughed out loud, a deep and booming laugh. A laugh that was all Jake. Chloe would never forget it. She laughed along with him. God, it was so good to see Jake happy again. At least for now, Chloe had made all his problems go away.

Chapter 71

    If Jake would have had a heart attack right at this very moment, it wouldn't have mattered. He would have died the happiest man on earth. She was beside him, making him laugh. At what should have been the darkest time in his life, she was making him forget it all and he was actually smiling. He looked at her long hair that fell around her face. A face so beautiful that no words could do it justice. And then there was her body. That breathtaking body that she had saved for him. No one else. She would never know what that meant to him. He reached for her, pulling her on top of him, tickling her.
    "What are you doing?" she giggled, trying to get away.
    "Don't you want to remember me again?" he teased, pulling her face towards his and kissing her.
    She laughed. "We just did it!"
    His eyes sparkled. "Ah, but my love…*this* is what all the girls were talking about!" He pushed himself against her thigh so that she could feel the full extent of his arousal.
    She playfully screamed, trying to pull her body away from him. But he was too strong, and he kept a tight hold on her. She laughed uncontrollably, wrestling with him. He laughed too, until he could hold out no longer. Whispering in her ear, he replied, "I want you,

Chloe. Over and over again. As much as you can handle." His voice was full of lust. He wasn't kidding.

Chloe stopped struggling. She looked him in the eyes. His words set her off. She bent down and kissed him hard on the lips. And for the rest of the night, they lived up to their word, making love as much as they possibly could. Until finally, they collapsed beside each other, completely exhausted.

Jake pulled her close to him, holding on tight. He kissed her bare shoulder and her cheek. She was tired. And so was he. He didn't want to close his eyes. Because he knew that when he opened them again, it would be time. Time to say goodbye to his everything. So he tried to stay awake. Tried not to miss another moment with her. But sleep came and seduced him. His eyes grew heavy. His body relaxed. His mind shut down and he drifted off to sleep.

Chapter 72

Daylight was peeking up over the pine trees. Birds were waking up and singing their morning songs. And Chloe was crying softly to herself. She was watching Jake sleeping peacefully while she wiped the tears that were streaming down her cheeks. How was she going to do this? How was she going to tell him goodbye? Her heart was breaking into a million pieces. A part of her was dying.

She stood and quietly dressed. And then she leaned down and kissed him on the cheek. He stirred and slowly opened his eyes. "It's time," she whispered to him.

He knew too. His face dropped as he quickly dressed.

Chloe walked a few feet away, staring off into the distance. A million thoughts ran through her head. God, she'd give ten years off of her life if she could just turn back time.

Jake came up behind her and touched her shoulder. She had been so strong, keeping it together. But now, a flood of emotions busted through the dam she had worked so hard to build. She turned and fell into his arms, crying. He was crying too, holding her as tight as he could.

"We'll be ok, Chloe. We're going to make it." He choked out the words.

"I keep telling myself this is the right thing to do," she cried against his chest.

He rubbed her hair. "It is, Chloe. Deep down, you know it is."

"Oh, it hurts! I love you so much!"

He kissed the top of her head. "I love you too, Chloe. I always will." They cried for a few minutes more as the birds chirped pretty melodies all around them.

Chloe pulled back and looked at Jake. "We're both realistic enough to know what could end up happening."

Jake nodded yes, not wanting to admit it. "You're right."

Chloe looked down and then back up at him. "I won't hold it against you if you won't hold it against me."

Jake smiled a bittersweet smile. "Never," he whispered to her. They kissed tenderly one last time. Reluctantly, they pulled apart. Chloe cried fiercely as she turned and got into her car that was all packed and ready to go. She started up the vehicle and drove away, her tears nearly blinding her. As much as she wanted to, she didn't dare look in the rearview mirror. Life without Jake lay up ahead. And she was driving straight towards it.

Ten Years Later…

Chapter 73

Jake Stevens walked with his good friend, Alex Carson, along the touristy streets of Montego Bay, Jamaica. They weaved their way in and out of all the people, stopping in at little shops. It was a beautiful day. The weather couldn't have been better. It was practically paradise on earth.

"I need to get Teresa something. A souvenir of some sort," replied Jake as he flipped through a rack of t-shirts with "Jamaica" emblazed on the front of them.

Alex grunted. "A t-shirt? Somehow, I don't think Teresa would appreciate that." Alex eyed some pretty women in bikini tops and floral print wraps that were several feet away.

"What's wrong with a t-shirt? I think they're kind of cool," laughed Jake. He noticed the women were smiling over at them. Alex was smiling back at them.

Jake just shook his head at his friend. Suddenly his cell phone rang. The display showed who was calling. He flipped it open and held it up to his ear. "Hi, honey. No, we're just checking out some of the shops. Yeah, it's great. I miss you too. Ok...I'll see you in a couple of days. Ok...love you too. Bye." He put the phone back into his pocket.

"Checking up on you again, huh?" joked Alex.

"Just calling to say hi," Jake defended himself.

Alex laughed. "She absolutely hates these trips of ours. It gets worse every year. Pretty soon, they'll be cut off all together."

Jake walked over to some shot glasses. "No they won't. It's been a tradition since college."

Alex eyed some books on Jamaica stacked on a bookshelf. "Yeah, well a lot of traditions get broken once the marriage gets finalized. Suddenly, she's calling all the shots."

Jake looked at his friend and laughed. "What makes you the expert on all this? I don't recall you ever being in a relationship for longer than a month!"

Alex ignored his comment and focused on some more beautiful women that just walked into the store.

Jake playfully punched him in the stomach. "Come on Casanova. Let's head over to another shop." Jake and Alex stepped out into the bright sun. They took in all the sights as they walked, thoroughly enjoying themselves. Jake looked past the town up towards the rolling hills that made up the rest of the island. Green foliage covered the landscape as far as the eye could see. It was breathtaking. Jake intended to go exploring up there before he left this place.

Jake and Alex spotted a small shop that looked like a good spot to pick up some cool memorabilia. They were busy discussing the evening's plans as Jake reached to open the door. He did not see someone coming out as he was trying to walk in. They nearly collided. Not looking up, Jake mumbled that he was sorry.

He lifted his eyes to this person and Jake froze dead in his tracks. Staring back at him, looking equally shell shocked, was a woman whose eyes looked distinctively familiar. *Holy shit!* It was Chloe. Jake blinked, thinking that he was imagining this. But she was still there, looking at him too, not able to speak either.

"Oh my God," Jake muttered out loud.

She lifted her hand to her mouth, still unable to speak.

Alex stood puzzled, wondering what was the matter. "Is there a problem?" he asked, trying to break the awkward silence.

THE DIAMOND HILLS

Jake couldn't tear his eyes away. Without looking at his friend, he managed to utter the words, "Alex, this is Chloe."

Chloe glanced away long enough to politely address Alex. "Hi," she softly replied, smiling at him.

Jesus Christ. It really was Chloe. That smile. That smile that Jake had buried somewhere deep in the back of his mind. It was here now. Right in front of him.

Alex laughed unbelievingly. "Wait a minute. Chloe Mayer? From high school?" He extended his hand which Chloe shook. Chloe looked surprised that Alex knew of her.

Jake finally snapped back to reality for a split second. "Yeah, I'm sorry. Chloe, this is Alex Carson."

She smiled again, sending chills down Jake's spine. "Nice to meet you," she told him.

Alex grinned. "You too! Wow." He eyed her, obviously pleased by what he saw. "So, you're the one."

His comment threw Chloe off. She got a funny look on her face as she glanced back at Jake. Jake fidgeted. Alex sensed the tension. He cleared his throat, half embarrassed. "Well, I'm just going to step in here and look around." He pointed towards the inside of the shop. He awkwardly slipped by them and told Jake he would be inside.

Jake nodded and then looked back at Chloe. They stood outside, just staring at each other, not believing that they were standing in front of each other. "Wow, Chloe…what are you doing here?" Jake broke the ice first.

She smiled at him. "A seminar. My firm sent me here."

Jake raised an eyebrow. "Your firm? What do you do?"

"A lawyer. I'm an attorney," she nervously replied.

Jake was stunned.

"And you? What are you doing here?" she asked, trying to take the focus off of her.

Jake looked towards the shop. "Alex and I. We go on these yearly trips. This year is Jamaica." He shrugged nervously. "Male bonding…" He grinned.

She grinned back. "Well, that's great." She locked eyes with him for a split second and then quickly looked down.

Jake's heart was racing. "How long are you here for?"

She looked back up. "Oh, I've got a red eye flight out of here tonight."

"Oh," was all he could say.

Chloe twisted the bag she was holding in her hands. "Well, I better get back to my seminar. Just thought I'd get a souvenir on my break." She opened up the bag and pulled out a t-shirt that had Jamaica emblazed across the front of it. "Cheesy huh?" she commented.

Jake stared at the t-shirt, not believing that after all these years, that connection was still there. He grinned, his blood pumping. "I think it's great!" he laughed.

She stuffed the t-shirt back in the sack. "Well, it was good seeing you, Jake."

Jake looked at her. She was even more beautiful than she was back then. She looked more mature, sophisticated, a woman who had come into her own. Her hair was still long, only a little lighter, perhaps bleached by the sun. She still had skin that looked like porcelain. Her body was still lean, athletic looking.

He stared into those deep dark brown eyes and suddenly, he was back there, in that other world. That world that they had created so long ago. Memories surfaced in his mind. Memories that he had buried. Now they were playing back like a reel of home movies. In an instant, he saw it all. The troubled childhood, his mother, her father, their friends, growing up together, that last night they shared at "The Diamond Hills". Everything. My God, did she see it all too? In him?

Chloe smiled and turned to walk away.

Something made him call out to her. "Chloe, would you like to grab a drink later on? Maybe after your seminar is over?"

She turned around and hesitated. "I don't know."

Jake shoved his hands in his pockets. "There's a little pub just down the street here." He paused. "It would be nice to catch up with an old friend."

Chloe twisted the sack in her hands again. She looked away and then back at him. "Sure. That would be nice." She nervously lifted her hand and waved at him. He waved back at her and watched as she turned and disappeared quickly amongst the crowds.

Chapter 74

Chloe peered into the window and caught sight of Jake sitting at the small table in the middle of the pub. He looked just as nervous as she was. Chloe moved back away from the window and leaned against the outside of the building, her hand over her racing heart. She closed her eyes. God, what was she doing here? She should just leave right now. Go back to her hotel room and then take off on her flight back to Boston.

But something inside her wouldn't let her do that. She stealthily peered into the window again. Jake ran his fingers through his hair, looking around at the few people that were in there. Man, talk about the biggest shock of her life running into him like that today. Never in a million years did she think she would ever see him again. Yet here he was, looking more gorgeous than ever. Older, wiser, a strong, confident man. Seeing him brought it all back. God, she thought she would never feel that way again. It scared her. It scared her because she remembered how it made her let go. Chloe took a deep breath and walked in.

He caught sight of her immediately, standing to greet her. He smiled at her. Oh that familiar smile that had always comforted her! Her mind flashed back to all those dark times he had helped her through with that smile. "Hi," she told him, grinning back at him, trying to conceal just how nervous she was. They both sat down. She glanced at him. He was tan, wearing a t-shirt and jeans. She could tell he still kept in very good shape. His arms were strong and muscular.

A waitress came up to take their drink order. They settled on a pitcher of beer. The waitress nodded and disappeared.

Jake focused on her. "How was your seminar?" he asked.

"Good," she commented. And then she smiled. "Boring."

He laughed gently. And then he asked, "So what kind of law do you practice?"

"I defend big companies and corporations that get sued by the general public." She grinned. "You know, product liability stuff."

Jake seemed impressed and genuinely interested. The waitress reappeared with two frosty mugs and a pitcher of frothy beer. Chloe watched as Jake poured both of their glasses. He slid her mug over to her.

She took a sip of the cold beer and watched as he did the same. "So, besides getting your testosterone fix by male bonding with your friend on yearly trips around the world, what else do you do?" She grinned at him when she saw he was amused by her question.

He looked down at his mug. "Actually, I'm in the middle of my second year of residency at Mount Sinai-Cedars Hospital in L.A." He looked back up at her to see her reaction.

She was shocked. "*Dr.* Jake Stevens?!" She smiled. "What kind of doctor?"

He grinned. "Cardio thoracic." He laughed gently. "Fancy name for a heart surgeon."

Chloe shook her head at him, covering her mouth with her hand in disbelief. She was so proud of him. "My God, Jake. That's wonderful," she told him.

He smiled at her. "You too. A high powered attorney. Wow." He looked down at his mug again and then back up at her, his face softening. "We made it, Chloe. We actually made it." His eyes burned into hers.

She saw it all again. The beatings, the heartaches, the hopelessness. The darkness that surrounded them. All they had was each other, praying they would make it through. The past was rushing back. He was seeing it too. Yet now, here they sat, two successful adults who had somehow climbed out of that darkness. "Yeah, we did," she replied softly.

He tore his eyes away, maybe to hide from her what she had already seen.

She took another drink. And then Chloe swallowed hard. She didn't want to ask, but she just had to know. "What about your mom, Jake?"

She could see a shadow pass over his eyes. But he kept a straight face and gripped his mug. "She passed away on her own a year after her accident."

Chloe hung her head for a minute, dealing with the sudden sadness she felt. "I'm so sorry, Jake." She lifted her head and looked at him, hoping he knew how she wished things could have been different, for everyone.

Jake sighed softly. "I'd like to think she's finally found peace and happiness." He smiled at Chloe.

Chloe nodded. "I'm sure she has." She smiled back at him, trying to lighten the mood again. And then out of nowhere, her next question came out. "So tell me, is there someone special?".

He grinned, nodding his head. "There is. Teresa."

Chloe smiled bigger, trying to conceal the sharp pain in her heart from the dagger that was being stabbed into it.

He looked directly at Chloe. "We're getting married in a month."

The dagger went in deeper. "Married! Wow! Congratulations! That's wonderful," Chloe lied.

Jake smiled. "Thank you." His eyes sparkled. But there was something missing in them. He hesitated for second. And then he grew serious again. "She wants to start a family right away."

Chloe listened, sensing that this bothered Jake.

"I'm not sure I'm ready for that yet," he confided. "It scares me. I don't know what kind of father I'll be."

THE DIAMOND HILLS

Chloe looked at Jake and knew. She knew his fear. She knew where it stemmed from. Maybe that's why he told her. She reached out and touched his hand with her fingertips. "Jake…you're going to make a wonderful father. I know you will."

He gave her a bittersweet smile. And then he spotted it. Her wedding ring. She quickly pulled her hand back.

"You're married?" he asked, his voice cracking slightly.

Chloe wished she could change the subject. And not talk about it but there was no avoiding it now. He had a right to know too. She looked down into her beer. "Yeah, two years now," she told him. Jake sat back in his chair, assessing her with his brown eyes. And then he smiled.

Chapter 75

He wasn't sure why it surprised him so much. But it did. What did he expect? It had been ten years. Jake continued to smile. "So tell me about him? What's his name? What does he do? What's he like?"

Chloe shook her head, avoiding his eyes. "It's over, Jake."

Her words made him shut up instantly. He could see the anguish on her face. She didn't want to talk about it. But she felt she needed to. Like she owed him that much. He didn't know what to say.

She continued to avoid his eyes, running her finger along the rim of her glass, around and around. "We're just waiting for the divorce to be finalized." She grunted, looking at the diamond on her left hand. "I don't know why I still wear this thing. Maybe I just don't want to admit that I failed."

Jake leaned forward. "What happened, Chloe?"

She looked up at him, the saddest look on her beautiful face. "He cheated on me." She held up her hand. "Wait, let me get that straight. He *cheats* on me."

Jake looked away. That old familiar anger began creeping into him. No one was supposed to hurt Chloe. *No one.*

Chloe continued. "But it's not all his fault."

Jake turned back to her.

She looked Jake in the eye. "I could never let him in, Jake. No matter how hard I tried or how much he wanted me to. I never let him in."

Jake swallowed hard. It was as if he was listening to himself. Teresa never knew the whole truth. He had told her bits and parts, enough to make her feel like he was sharing a part of his past with her. But he never let her in either. Not completely.

Guilt crept over Jake. It was crazy. After all these years, he still felt responsible. Like he should have done something. He was always supposed to be the protector. "I'm so sorry, Chloe. I should have been there for you."

It was Chloe's turn to smile a bittersweet smile. "Don't apologize, Jake."

Jake shook his head. "I don't know what happened, Chloe. I don't know how we lost each other."

Chloe reached for his arm, touching it with her fingertips. "Hey, we can sit here all day wondering what went wrong. Going back to analyze what happened, why we drifted apart and didn't keep in touch. The reasons all lead to dead ends."

Jake looked up at her. He understood exactly what she was saying. How many times had he tried to go back for peace of mind? He never could find a definitive answer.

She smiled at him. "Water under the bridge, right?....As the old saying goes."

He smiled at her. She was still amazing. Still trying to find the bright side of things. Still trying to make him smile. He remembered they had promised not to hold it against each other. That was one promise they kept. She held no grudges. He didn't either.

She leaned back and brought the mug up to her lips. He watched her, taking her all in. Funny how he felt so comfortable now. They were picking up right where they left off. Jesus, he was sure they had shared more with each other in 15 minutes then they ever had with their significant others. It scared Jake. He knew it was wrong but he didn't want it to stop.

He took a huge swallow from his glass. And then an idea struck him. "Come on, I want to show you something." He stood up.

Chloe laughed and stood up too. "What, are we seven again?"

He grinned, his heart pounding. He felt like he *was* seven again. The same excitement. The same exhilaration. They walked out of the pub and up the street a ways. He pointed to a convertible Porsche. "Get in, we're going for a drive."

Chloe did as he said. "Is this one of your toys?"

Jake started up the vehicle and revved up the engine. "Rent a car. But one day…I plan on having three!" He shifted the gear shift and took off as Chloe laughed out loud.

They headed up a winding road that led up towards the rolling hills. The hills slowly turned into small mountains that made up the rest of the island of Jamaica. Green trees native to the area blanketed the landscape on both sides of the road. It was breathtaking. Every now and then, Jake would steal glances at Chloe. She looked so happy, smiling, taking in everything around her. Her long hair whipped around as the wind blew through it. She seemed to have forgotten about her impending divorce and other problems she might have had. Her face glowed. She was looking at him, laughing as he shifted gears. They climbed higher and deeper into the native forest. She was so beautiful. God, he shouldn't be looking at her like that, but she was. So beautiful.

And then she did it. She turned to him, her eyes sparkling. Her pretty mouth opened and she said it; familiar words he had heard before. "Faster, Jake! Go faster!"

He was back there. With her. Right beside him like she was now. Running from the cops, knowing that whatever happened, it didn't matter. They had each other. And that was all they needed. She was looking at him now, that wildness in her eyes. She was back there too. Reliving that time in their lives that neither of them had forgotten. Another buried memory resurfacing.

Jake smiled and pushed down on the accelerator. Chloe hollered at the top of her lungs, standing on top of the seat and sitting on the trunk of the Porsche. She arched her head back and laughed a deep laugh. Jake knew then that she had not laughed like that in a long time. He was mesmerized as he watched the wind whip around her. Chloe was letting go.

He felt himself letting go too. God it felt so good. He felt so alive and free. She was laughing, smiling, making him laugh too. He didn't want this ride to end. Jake could have stayed on it forever.

They pulled up to a clearing. A small waterfall splashed into a little pool of water. Chloe got out and walked up to the edge. He came up beside her, staring at the huge cliffs above them. Out of nowhere, the question came out. "Do you still have the nightmares, Chloe?"

She turned to him, startled at first. But then her eyes told him he was still the only one who knew about them. "Every now and then. But not like before." She looked down at the ground. "You were right." She looked at him again.

He turned and faced her.

"They never go away completely. I've just learned to deal with them better," she replied. She gave him a warm smile. For a split second, Jake felt her tenderness again. She was silently telling him thank you.

Another moment was passing between them. Jake nervously looked back up at the cliffs. And then he spotted the fallen log. "Hey look at that." He pointed to it. "Does that look familiar or what?"

She saw it too and smiled.

He eyed her. "You still got it in you?"

She eyed him back, grinning. "Absolutely!" She laughed and took off running. He followed her, his heart racing. He watched as she jumped effortlessly onto the log, balancing her lean body on it and walking on it like she had done it forever. He climbed aboard as well. They headed out towards the middle of it until they were standing high above a rushing stream.

Jake watched as Chloe gracefully turned and faced him. She extended her hand. He took it, feeling the same electricity shoot up his arm that he felt all those years ago. She began walking backward, not looking down or around, but focusing only on him.

He slowly followed her, feeling the cool breeze on his face and the rumble of the stream underneath his feet. She wasn't scared. Neither was he. They had done this so many times before.

She was reading his mind. "Do you remember the first time?" she asked.

He nodded, not letting go of her hand. "The fog was so thick. We couldn't see how far it was to the bottom."

She smiled, clearly impressed that he was recalling all the details. "But we said it didn't matter. If we fell, at least we'd fall together." Her eyes shined as the memory of being a kid again came rushing back.

Jake stared at her. God the world they had created back then just to cope. To make it through. Life was so dark that falling, possibly to their deaths, didn't matter. As long as they had each other, they would be ok. "I remember," he softly replied.

They stood, still holding hands. Not afraid to fall. *Just hold onto each other and fall*... Jake felt her hand slipping out of his grasp. She was moving on, making her way skillfully along the log towards the other end. A mountain lion, a swift deer. Isn't that what they had always thought she was like? It was nice to see that some things didn't change. He smiled to himself, following her lead.

"Look, Jake!" she called over her shoulder. "Someone attached this vine to the top of that tree branch." She held onto it.

He looked ahead. She was grasping onto it with both hands. He eyed the branch that it was tied to. And then he scanned the direction it would take if someone swung on it. He caught up to her. She was grinning, her eyes glowing again. She was finding her escape. Leaving behind all the bullshit the last several years had dealt her. More importantly, she was sharing with him again. God it felt so good. Chloe was letting him in. No one else. Just him. Just like it always had been. "You're crazy, Chloe," he laughed.

She threw her head back and laughed. "Come on, Jake! You know you want to!" she taunted.

She had no idea... Jake watched as her toned arms gripped the vine. In an athletic swoop, she jumped up and off the log, wrapping her legs around the vine at the ankles. She screamed an exhilarated scream as she sailed through the air, over and across the flowing stream, clear to the other side of the bank. She landed like a pro on a bed of green grass flat on her feet.

Jake couldn't stop laughing. Man, he was a kid too. She swung the vine back towards him. He caught it, balancing himself on the log. He hadn't done this in years. She was bringing it all back out. Like no one else could. Jake jumped off, flying through the air, feeling himself floating. She was watching, waiting for him on the other side. Just like in his mind. Always waiting…

He landed on his feet too, his heart thudding hard in his chest. Chloe jumped up and down, laughing, cheering him on. She was high. As high as he was. She grabbed his hand again, pulling him along as she took off running. "Come on Jake! Let's see what's over here."

Jake followed her. Through every nook and cranny of the underbrush and trees. On top of every ledge and cliff. They took it all in, not missing a thing. Seven years old. Exploring. Just the two of them. Nothing else mattered. Jake kept going back. He knew she was back there too.

They talked and laughed. Forgetting. Forgetting that ten long years had passed. Forgetting that they had missed out on each other lives. They were back there again, picking up right where they left off.

Jake would stop every now and then and take her all in. She was still Chloe. Beautiful, amazing. My God, what had happened? How could they have let it happen?

The sun was beginning to set, bringing them back to reality. To the present. He didn't want it to end. She didn't either. But they weren't seven. They were adults. Jake sighed. "We better head back."

Chloe sighed too. "You're right." They both slowly made their way back to the car.

Chapter 76

Ever so slowly, Jake drove the Porsche down the hill. Chloe turned and looked at him. He was right here beside her. She had dreamed of this. A secret she had kept from Tom, her soon to be ex-husband. One of many secrets she had kept locked away deep inside of her. Chloe wanted to reach out now. And touch Jake. Just once. She wanted to feel it again. The love. That amazing love they had once shared. Did he feel it too?

He turned to her then, the breeze moving his dark hair around. She had to catch her breath. My God, it was still there. The butterflies.

"Have you been back, Chloe?" he asked.

She stared at him, still trying to catch her breath.

"Home," he continued. He faced the road again. "To 'The Diamond Hills'?"

She shook her head no. "What about you?" she asked.

He gripped the steering wheel with his left hand. "I passed through several years ago. They've built a subdivision there now. Houses as far as you can see."

"Wow!" Chloe smiled. "I wonder where the teenagers go to party nowadays?"

Jake laughed. "I don't know." Chloe could tell he was recalling those crazy nights they had all spent hanging out.

"Funny how things change," Chloe replied. Bittersweet feelings surfaced again. Old memories. Recalling the past.

Jake smiled. "Yeah," he replied. "Everything changes." And then he faced her again. "Except for our secret hiding place. It's still there."

Chloe looked at him, her heart racing.

"They haven't found it yet," he softly replied, looking deep into her eyes. He had gone back there. Had purposely scouted it out. Had seen that their special place was one thing time hadn't touched. It still held all the memories.

Did it still mean the world to him like it did to her? She remembered everything they had shared there. Especially that last night. She would never forget it.

Jake was trying to read her. She quickly looked away, afraid to reveal what she was feeling. It wasn't right. They had moved on. They had to move on now.

Jake pulled up in front of her hotel. They sat beside each other, an awkward silence passing between them. Chloe wanted to tell him so much. But she knew she couldn't tell him anything. And so she kept quiet, looking up at the window of her third story hotel room. Before the sun would rise again, she would be gone. Back to her life in Boston where she would continue to wait patiently for the divorce to be finalized. And then what?

"I had so much fun today, Jake." She turned to him and smiled. "Thank you," she told him. And she hoped he knew she wasn't just thanking him for the day. She was thanking him for everything.

Jake didn't speak. He seemed at a loss for words.

Chloe felt the sadness creep over her. She quickly opened the car door to get out.

Jake called out to her. "Chloe!"

Her heart skipped a beat. Why was he prolonging this? It was killing her. She turned around.

He sat up on the back hood of the car, his tanned skin glowing as dusk began to fall all around them. She had never seen a more amazing sight.

"Alex and I are going to a little bar on the other side of town. He's got some friends coming in. I don't know any of them."

It was her turn not to speak. She simply stood there and stared at him. Chloe was dying inside. But at the same time, the butterflies were fluttering again.

He knew her hesitation. Her anguish. He could read her like an open book. "We don't have to talk about the past….or the future. We'll just have fun." He was begging. She could see it in his eyes. He wanted one last moment with her too. Before they had to say goodbye forever.

Chloe shifted from one foot to the other, looking nervously around at the cars that drove up and down the road. He was watching her, waiting for her response. It was so wrong. They both knew it. It would lead to nowhere. Another dead end road. But she couldn't stop herself. He did that to her. Made her lose control. She looked into his eyes. They were still pleading with her. "Ok, what's the name of the bar? I'll meet you there."

He couldn't stop smiling as she watched him drive away. Chloe shook her head and headed inside her hotel. Once again, she was asking herself what in the hell was she doing? But this time, she couldn't stop smiling either.

Chapter 77

    Jake had already forgotten all of the names of the people that Alex had introduced him to. Apparently, they were all close friends and extremely happy to meet up with Alex. They didn't waste any time buying a round of drinks and raising the roof off of the little bar that sat on the edge of Montego Bay. Everyone who was anyone seemed to be here. Beautiful women filled the place, dancing on the dance floor to hip music, hanging out at the bar, flirting with all the men. Alex was in heaven. Jake was in hell, hoping and praying that Chloe would show. His mind was riddled with guilt. Jesus, he was engaged to be married in a month. Yet here he was not even thinking of Teresa. He had talked to her back at his hotel room before he showed up here. Was it to ease his conscience? He didn't know. He didn't know anything anymore. His world had suddenly turned upside down. But he couldn't help it. He wanted to be here. He wanted Chloe to be here too.

    Jake slugged back the shot that Alex handed him. Thank God Alex was already pretty intoxicated. He hoped Alex couldn't see how messed up he was inside. He avoided giving any details when Alex asked about his afternoon with Chloe. Jake just offered short, to the point answers, downplaying the amazing time he experienced.

"Drink up, buddy. This is our last night in paradise. Make the most of it!" hollered Alex. He handed Jake another shot and turned his attention to a gorgeous blonde that strolled by the two of them.

Jake swallowed the liquor, closing his eyes as it burned going down his throat. The loud music pulsed in his ears. The laughter from the crowds of people echoed in his head. He slammed the shot glass down on the bar and turned towards the door. It swung open. Jake saw Chloe walk through it and his jaw dropped. Her long hair was wild around her face. Her earrings dangled just above her exposed shoulders. She wore a tight tank top and even tighter jeans. Her body was still athletic and toned. She looked absolutely amazing.

She looked around the bar, searching for him. And then she spotted him and smiled. It radiated throughout the whole room. Jake stood frozen, transfixed by her beauty. Alex noticed the trance like state Jake was in and looked to see what was the cause of it. He nearly dropped his drink when he saw her. "Wow, she's hot!" was his graceful response.

Jake snapped back to reality for a split second to glare at his drunk friend.

Alex cleared his throat. "I-I mean, she's looks very nice."

Chloe walked up to them. Jake could not contain himself. He smiled from ear to ear.

"Hi," she replied.

"Hi," he responded back.

She stepped forward and hugged him. It nearly knocked him to his feet because it felt so good. He circled his arms around her small frame, trying to control his racing heart. God it had been so long since he felt her like this. He wanted to linger. But he knew it was wrong. They pulled apart. She smiled at Alex and told him hello.

Alex extended his hand. She graciously gave him hers. He pulled it up to his lips and kissed the top of her knuckles. Chloe giggled at his inebriation. Jake watched her face glowing, mesmerized by her charm. Alex and Chloe made small talk while Jake ordered them

THE DIAMOND HILLS

some drinks. They found a table and sat down. Chloe looked around at the scene. "It's crazy in here tonight."

"Yes it is!" hollered Alex. "So drink up, Chloe!" He pushed her drink towards her.

She laughed. "Are you trying to get me drunk, Alex?" she jokingly asked.

"You bet I am!" he slurred.

Chloe laughed harder, looking at Jake. Jake shook his head, staring back at his wild friend. But Chloe took her drink and downed it.

Alex's eyes grew big. "Wow, you don't mess around." He lifted his hand to the passing waitress and told her to bring more drinks.

Over the next hour, the three talked and laughed while downing drink after drink. Jake felt so at ease. He wasn't thinking about anything. The only thing on his mind was that he was having the time of his life. He could tell Chloe felt the same. She was cutting up, letting loose and obviously charming the heck out of Alex. He knew Alex was impressed at how easy it was to talk to Chloe. She was down to earth, witty and sincere. She literally had Alex in stitches with one of her funny stories. Alex stood up from the table, holding his side. "I'm gonna piss my pants," he managed to choke out. "I'll be right back." He excused himself and headed to the bathroom.

Chloe turned her attention to Jake. Jake scanned her face. So sexy, so captivating. He nervously gripped his drink. "Are you having fun, Chloe?"

She grinned. "Yeah, I am." She scanned his face too. Another moment. They were happening again. And they shouldn't be. Both of them knew it. Chloe looked away.

An upbeat song began playing. Jake didn't want her to feel uncomfortable. He had told her they were here to have fun. He reached for her hand. "Come on, let's go dance."

She seemed to appreciate the friendly gesture. They headed out to the dance floor that was packed with people. Jake had never been the best dancer. But liquor somehow made him think he was. Chloe laughed at him as he threw his arms into the air, shaking his hips.

She didn't seem to care that he was making an absolute fool out of himself. In fact, she joined in on his antics, acting silly herself. People began looking at them. Chloe and Jake couldn't have cared less. They were having fun. So much fun that they stayed out on the dance floor and danced like idiots for the next several blocks of music.

Jake couldn't believe it. He felt so alive. So at home. So right. God, it was so wrong. But it felt so right. She was with him. He was with her. Everyone around them had disappeared. Was this where he was supposed to be? After all these years...did he come full circle?

The song ended and Chloe dragged him off the dance floor. "No more!" she told him. "I'm about to die." They plopped down into their chairs, laughing, looking into each other's eyes, downing more drinks. Not realizing that they were being watched.

Chapter 78

Alex was drunk. But he was sober enough to see that his friend was in trouble. Serious trouble. From the moment Jake had bumped into Chloe, Alex could see that's Jake's world had turned upside down. His past had suddenly collided head on with his present and it was about to affect his future. Jake thought it wasn't noticeable. But Alex was no idiot. He could see it all transpiring right in front of his eyes. Alex watched Jake and Chloe at the table as they talked, laughed, and looked at each other in that way. It was as if nothing else existed. They were in their own world.

Alex had known Jake for about eight years now. He considered Jake one of his best friends. He felt he knew Jake pretty well. Alex had been there for all his ups and downs through college, medical school and now their residencies. He had witnessed all of Jake's relationships with countless past girlfriends and of course, now with Teresa, Jake's fiancé. But through all of that, he had never seen what he was seeing now. The way Jake was looking at Chloe, Alex had never seen Jake look at any woman like that, not even Teresa. It worried Alex. What was his friend getting himself into? Was he setting himself up to getting hurt like he did all those years ago? Worse yet, was he going to end up hurting someone else?

Alex took a swallow from his drink, not taking his eyes away from Jake and Chloe. They were talking about something and laughing like they had been hanging out with each other forever. Two old friends picking up right where they left off. Alex shook his head. "I hope you know what the hell you're doing, buddy," Alex whispered to himself under his breath.

Chapter 79

Chloe was losing track of time. She and Jake had been talking about everything and nothing at all. Only with Jake was that possible. And he had kept true to his word. They didn't speak of the past and they didn't bring up the future. They just…talked. She had closed herself off for so long. It felt good to open up again. He made her feel safe. Like she could tell him anything. Oh, how she wished it could go on forever. She missed this. She missed him.

Chloe glanced at her watch. It wouldn't be long now. The inevitable would happen. She couldn't hide the sadness in her eyes. And neither could he. He nervously ran his fingers through his hair.

"I know I said we wouldn't talk about the past. But running into you again…I can't help but kick myself. Chloe…I missed the last ten years of your life. I could have done so much more then I did." Jake looked down at his hands. "Everything we went through as kids…growing up, the shit we dealt with…I feel like I've let you down." Amazingly, his eyes began to water slightly. He really did feel bad about letting what they had slip away.

Chloe took his hand in hers. She still knew his heart and the person he was. "Always my protector. Even after all these years." She smiled at him tenderly. "Jake, don't you know? I wouldn't be here right now if it weren't for you. You saved my life. You saved *me.*" She reached out and grazed his cheek with her hand. My God. She still loved him. She had never stopped. "So don't ever feel you've let me down."

Jake looked at her, his eyes watering even more with her words. She knew he understood her. He squeezed her hand and led her to the dance floor as a sad love song began playing. "Dance with me one last time, Chloe….before we have to say goodbye," Jake whispered. He was crying silently now, pulling her close to him.

Chloe began crying too, tears streaming down her face. She held onto him, feeling his strong arms around her. Closing her eyes, her mind took her back to that last night at the "Diamond Hills", where they had shared their love for each other. She remembered the stars, the cool breeze on their bodies, the way Jake made love to her over and over again. How she had dreamed of that night so many times. Fantasized about being in his embrace again. And now here she was, right where she wanted to be. But she couldn't have him. She couldn't tell him that she still loved him. She knew soon, she would have to let him go…again. And that's why the tears wouldn't stop flowing.

Chapter 80

    Jake had never felt so emotionally torn. He felt sad. He felt angry. Angry at himself. Even angry at Chloe. Why did she have to come back into his life? Why now? He had moved on, started a new life, found someone else to love. All memories of Chloe and what they had were shoved somewhere to the back of his mind, hidden in the deepest recesses of his brain. That was the only way he knew how to cope. How to deal with the loss of the one true love of his life. And just when he thought he was ok, she had to come back. And damn, she was still Chloe! Still the same amazing, beautiful, thoughtful, kind person he had fallen so hard for all those years ago. How long had he loved her? Maybe since they were little kids when all they had was each other to cling to. All he knew was that she had always had him…completely. His heart, his soul, his everything. Why did they have to end up like this? In a place where both of their hands were tied. Where they were both about to face another major heartache? It was hurting like hell. All over again. And there wasn't a damn thing either of them could do about it.

    The clock was ticking. Jake could hear it in his head. It was deafening. He wanted to scream. Wanted to push her away. Wanted to pull her close. Wanted to turn back time. Wanted to make it all go away. It was killing him inside. Just like he knew it was killing her inside too.

He pulled back and stared her in the eyes. When it was all said and done, all they had left was this moment. This very moment right now in each others arms. She knew it too. He didn't have to say a word. His sad eyes told her everything he wanted to say. And just like always, she understood him perfectly. That unbreakable bond. It was still there.

Jake pressed his forehead against hers, closing his eyes, feeling her breath upon his lips. So close, so untouchable. He couldn't bear to do it. As much as he wanted to, he knew it wasn't right. She was holding back too, trying like hell to do the right thing, her body quivering against his. He could hear her silently screaming, feeling the same anguish he was feeling, knowing the same questions were replaying over and over in her mind. He held her face with both of his hands. She quietly cried as they slowly swayed to the soft music that filled the little bar in the middle of paradise on earth. Jake cried too, holding onto her for dear life. Even though people were all around them, they were all alone. In that place that was all theirs. The world they had created so long ago. And for as long as the song would let them, they were going to stay right there.

Chapter 81

As the music began to fade, Chloe pulled away. It was time. There was no stopping it now. Too much had happened. Life had taken them on different paths. They couldn't turn back. He was crying. It didn't matter that people were starting to stare. He was crying.

"I have to go," Chloe managed to whisper to him. He didn't want to stop holding her hands. She let him pull her in one last time. With all her might, she hugged him, burning this moment into her brain, just like all the others. Her heart was shattering into a million pieces. She wanted to scream at the top of her lungs. A part of her was dying all over again. She looked him in the eyes and touched his cheek. "I wish you all the best, Jake." She wiped the tears from her eyes. Forcing a weak smile on her sad face, she managed to pull away one last time and walk away. *One foot in front of the other. You can do it.* Chloe walked away. She walked further and further away from Jake. And just like that, he was gone. And Chloe never, ever turned around.

Chapter 82

"What can I get you to drink?" asked the flight attendant. Jake didn't hear her. He was staring out the window of the plane that was soaring 30,000 feet in the air.

Alex knew it was pointless to try and get Jake's attention. "I'm sorry," he told the flight attendant. "Nothing for us right now. Thank you." She nodded and went to the next aisle.

Alex turned back towards Jake. Chloe's plane left at 2 this morning. Jake never slept. He just holed himself up in his hotel room until Alex banged on his door to tell him it was time to head to the airport. They were flying home, back to their lives. And Jake looked like hell.

"Come on, dude. You can't do this," he told Jake.

Jake barely took his eyes from the clouds outside his window. He didn't say a word.

Alex sighed. "You're getting married in a month."

Jake looked down at his hands that sat in his lap. "I know that," he barely muttered. And then he looked back out the window.

Alex ran his fingers through his hair. "Look, I know you and Chloe went through a lot of shit growing up…"

Jake snapped his head back at Alex and glared at him. "No one knows what we went through. No one!" he shouted.

Alex held up his hands to calm him. "Ok, ok!" Alex looked around at the other passengers, hoping they hadn't caused a scene. He turned back to Jake and lowered his voice. "You guys had something special. Something no one could ever understand. I get that. But you were kids. That was a long time ago. You two are different people now. You can't let one night dictate the rest of your life." Alex hoped Jake was even hearing him. He continued. "And Teresa. She's been there right by your side for the last three years."

Jake looked down at his hands again. "I know that too."

"You know as much as I bag on her, Teresa's a good person. She doesn't deserve this."

Jake turned to his friend. His eyes pleaded with Alex for an answer. A solution to this debacle he was in. "I love Teresa, Alex. You know I do. But what if this chance meeting with Chloe was meant to tell me something?"

Alex cleared his throat and leaned in. "Do you still love her? Chloe? Do you still love her?"

Jake didn't say a word. He didn't have to. His eyes radiated the answer.

Alex leaned back against his seat and he sighed heavily. "Jesus, Jake. You never stopped, did you?"

Jake looked out the window again.

Alex put his hand on Jake's shoulder. He knew his friend was in serious trouble. His whole world was crumbling right before his eyes. And no one could help him. This was something he was going to have to figure out for himself. "As your friend, I hope you know I'll never tell Teresa about any of this." He paused. "But I hope you think long and hard about this, Jake. About what you're contemplating and about what you could possibly be losing."

Jake turned to him then.

Alex looked him square in the eyes. "I know in the end…you'll do the right thing."

Epilogue…

    The tiny newborn baby squirmed and kicked in its little warming bed, its fists flailing all around. Well developed lungs produced newborn wails that echoed through the whole hospital room bringing happy grins to all of the medical staff. Another healthy birth.
    The nurse swaddled the baby up in a blanket. She walked over to the man who stood in awe of it. "Would you like to hold your son, Dr. Stevens?" She grinned as she handed the little bundle towards Jake. With shaking arms, Jake took the baby, cradling him ever so gently. He stared down at his perfect little face. "Hello, Timothy," he whispered. The baby stopped crying and stared up at his father's face. Jake looked up at the nurse, amazed that his son recognized his voice. The nurse smiled even bigger. "He already knows who his daddy is," she replied. Jake looked back down at Timothy's face. My God. He was beautiful. So perfect. So precious. His eyes were wide open, looking up at Jake, studying him. Jake kissed him on the forehead, his heart filling up with so much love. He was a father now. He was responsible for this little person in his arms. Jake was terrified. And exhilarated at the same time. How could he even describe it?

Another nurse walked in and touched Jake on the shoulder. "There are some people out there who have been patiently waiting for you all day." She smiled at him too, seeing the absolute love Jake already had for this precious little bundle of joy.

Jake grinned. "Oh, that's my family," he told her. Jake turned towards his wife who was being tended to by the medical staff.

"Don't worry. She'll be alright," the nurse reassured him. She patted him on the back.

Jake nodded and headed out of the room and began walking down the long hall towards the waiting area. He couldn't tear his eyes away from his son. The baby just simply stared up at him, still studying his features. Jake couldn't believe this was happening. He knew he would protect this child, love him unconditionally, give him all the things he never had. Jake thought of his own father. The father that never wanted him. That abused him. That neglected him. That never loved him. As Jake looked at his own son, he made a vow to himself right then and there that the cycle would be broken. It would end with him. He would be the one to change things. Make it right.

Jake entered the waiting room, smiling from ear to ear as he looked at the three members of his family. Alex, Brad and Jeff all stood up and rushed over to him. They stood in awe too of the little boy cradled in Jake's arms. "He's amazing," replied Brad.

"Can I hold him?" asked Jeff. Jake, Alex and Brad all stared at Jeff. They couldn't believe he had just asked that.

Jake smiled and nodded. He handed his son over to Jeff who cuddled the baby like he had done it forever. Gone was the wild, crazy kid who had always liked to raise hell. In his place stood a mature, successful man who looked like he couldn't wait to have a child of his own one day.

Alex patted Jake on the back. "Congratulations, Jake! You're a dad now!"

"Thank you!"

Brad grinned. "So how is she?" he asked nodding towards the area Jake had just come from.

THE DIAMOND HILLS

"She's ok. It was a long labor but she did it. She's pretty exhausted."

Jeff looked up. "Well you look pretty exhausted yourself." He kissed the baby and handed him back to Jake.

Brad nodded in agreement. "Yeah, Jeff and I need to get back to the office anyway. It seems that place can't run without us there."

Jake smiled as he looked at his two old friends. He was so proud of them. They were partners in an extremely successful internet based company they both had co-founded. Business was literally booming for them, allowing them to live in the fast lane. Yet when it counted, they had all found each other again, just like they had promised. Within a year, Brad and Jeff had relocated to where Jake was at, stating that life was too short to not be near best friends. They fell right into Jake and Alex's life, getting along like brothers.

Alex rubbed Timothy's little head. "Yeah, I need to get back to my clinic. The patients are probably lined up outside the door."

Jake looked at all of his friends. They were the greatest friends a guy could have. They meant the world to him. "Thanks guys. For being here."

They all nodded. "Get some rest, Jake. Call us when you all get settled in at home," replied Brad. They congratulated him again and told him good bye as they all left.

Jake took his son and headed back towards the hospital room. He went and sat down at the edge of his wife's bed. He looked at her. She was exhausted. But she radiated as she stared at the little baby. God he loved her. They had created this life together. Timothy was a part of both of them. Knowing that made him love her even more. They were forever bonded by this perfect little miracle. He looked in her tired eyes and knew he was right where he should be. Not a doubt in his mind.

Jake looked back down at Timothy. The baby began sucking on his tiny fingers. Jake smiled. He kissed him on the forehead again. And then in a soft voice, he spoke to the baby. "I'm going to love you and hug you and throw you birthday parties and take you to the zoo. And I'm never, ever going to leave you." Jake looked back up at his wife.

She just stared at him, his words bringing tears to her eyes. "You remembered that?" she whispered, her voice shaking.

Jake leaned over and kissed Chloe on the lips. He looked her deep in the eyes and then smiled. "How could I ever forget?"